Garden of Eden Anthology

Biblical Legends Anthology Series

Edited by

Allen Taylor

Copyright © 2014 Garden Gnome Publications

First Printing, February 2014
Second Printing, May 2023

**Cover art by
Alexandre Rito**
All rights reserved.

ISBN: 978-1535509411; 1535509414

The garden gnomes would sincerely like to connect with you at our social media outposts. Please, drop on by!

Follow our editor on Twitter (https://twitter.com/allen_taylor), Hive (https://hive.blog/@allentaylor), and Paragraph https://paragraph.xyz/@tayloredcontent.

Contents and Discontents

This anthology is dedicated to anyone and everyone who has ever looked, felt, tasted, or smelled like a garden gnome and their relatives, owners, assigns, foot props, and nearby tree stumps.

ALPHA

ALLEN TAYLOR

An anthology is like a box of chocolates. You put a call out and see what happens. In the case of the Garden of Eden, I was pleasantly surprised.

For all the trouble I went through to write the rules and post them, many of the submissions I received were in clear violation. No Adam and Eve, and for dear God's sake, no serpents. In this collection of stories, we have all three. I think you'll agree, the stories are spectacular.

We have other characters, too.

Roaches, for instance. Water Rats. Angels. Gnomes. And even the Tree itself. Yes, *that* tree. *The* tree. As a character.

Hey, I asked for absurdity. And, boy, did I get it.

Of course, the challenges of planning and publishing an anthology are tremendous. The joys no less. Right from the beginning, I had a cheerleader. As soon as she heard about my plans to take submissions for a Garden of Eden anthology, AmyBeth Inverness got excited. She was more excited than I was. It didn't bother me that she submitted her story, "The Genesis of the Incorporeum," in the final hour. It's only fitting that it should lead the short story section. Not because it is good - it is that (read it for yourself!) - but because it sets the pace for what is to follow. There's not a single disappointment.

If you find convenient serendipities here, don't be surprised. For instance, it's no accident that the first story you'll read is by an author named Adam.

My vision from the beginning was crisp, like a well-pruned garden leaf. I had established early on that I was going to publish a handful of flash fiction stories, a few short stories, one poem, and one essay. I figured I'd get plenty of fiction pieces, and I did. Alas, I could not publish them all.

Getting poetry and essay submissions proved to be somewhat more challenging. I wanted to publish two poems, but I stuck with my original vision and broke someone's heart. As far as essays go, I didn't get one submission. Not to be beat, I asked John Vicary if I could publish his flash fiction story "Before Dawn Can Wake Us" as an essay instead. It had the perfect flavor of what I had in mind for that section, aptly titled OMEGA.

As you read, you can easily envision the narrator delivering this monologue from a park bench anywhere in the world today. Right now, even.

One question that I often encounter as I discuss the Biblical Legends Anthology Series with potential readers is, "Does it remain true to the Bible?" The answer is proverbial. It depends.

Some readers want to know if all the stories adhere to a strict Evangelical interpretation of events in the Bible. In that case, the answer is *no, they do not.* Some readers may want to know if the stories are biblical in the sense that they convey any spiritual values. Some of them do. But not all of them. And let's not forget that here, in the 21st century, we can't even get people to agree on what "spiritual values" are, but I'll refrain from going down that road. The truest way to answer the question is to say that some of the writers approached their stories from a Christian perspective while others did not. To be honest, I didn't ask anyone about their background. I just wanted well-told stories and literary gems. If that sounds blasphemous, please forgive me.

But I do ask for your honest assessment. Not of me, but of the stories within. Give them a read. I'm sure you'll like some and not care for others. After all, that's what anthologies are about—the delivery of literary nuggets in a softshell.

Therefore, without further ado, I present to you these biblical (and not-so-biblical) nuggets.

FLASH FICTIONS

IN THE BEGINNING WE DID HAVE SOMEONE ON THE GROUND

ADAM MAC

Roaches. We were simply called "roaches," though perhaps even then we should have been called "cockroaches." our tradition is that only the male figures into historical accounts. The progenitor of our species, ed, lived googol^googol generations ago. In the beginning, he was there in the garden of Eden, notwithstanding the apocryphal accounts of people.

In the garden, Ed hovered about openly on the lookout for crumbs and dribbles. Back then, there were no cupboards to hide in and no sudden bright lights to skitter away from. And we weren't afflicted with the demeaning stereotype propagated by bigoted speciesists, like K. So, in the beginning, Adam and eve were pretty relaxed with ed around, and ed, for his part, was usually pretty good about not crawling on their naked bodies when they were following god's detailed instructions on how to make Cain and Abel.

Things were ideal—they'd never been better. On the other hand, since there was no comparison, some detractors point out that they'd never been worse. Ed, the father of our race, was an optimist, though. From him, we learned that a crumb under foot is better than ....

That part has always puzzled us. Even our intellectuals are baffled. Anyway, Ed, regarded as methuselah by generations of his progeny, who were also his contemporaries, promised that through his descendants he would live forever, come hell or high water. Noah gave us a helping hand on the high-water thing, albeit unwittingly, and it's received wisdom among Adam's and eve's offspring that we — alone — will survive hell.

Back to the story.

It was a perfect world. Absolutely perfect. Better than malibu. Then one day, eve got a little tired and bored with the straight and narrow and scampered over to the apple tree, which was a no-no.

Ed followed. Of course, Winston was there and he wooed and wowed eve and persuaded her to squeeze the apple hard and drink the liquid. You have to remember that Adam and Eve were bigger and stronger, and even better looking, than people today. Lots more body hair and a wonderfully

4

sloped forehead. Squeezing the juice out of an apple by hand was no big deal. But their brains were still mostly dormant. So even though Eve and Adam looked to the heavens for guidance, eve didn't register the anomaly of the rumbling in the clouds when she had her first swallow. Ed, too, was in the moment. From his perspective, this was sweet.

Eve took another apple—just one. The abundance of food meant that Adam and Eve didn't have to worry about hunting and gathering and storing. Every day, the items on the menu just fell into place ... literally. Survival-type skills were a thing of the future, which itself was a thing of the future since "everything" was now.

Eve wrung the apple until it was dry pulp and put the juice in a huge banana leaf. She carried it to Adam, who was very thirsty by late afternoon, having lain in the hot sun for hours, not comprehending why his skin was red and burning. Ed was there, too. He was still hanging around, although, by this point, he was bloated—as big as the mouse eve was finally going to meet tomorrow morning.

Adam loved the apple juice, and eve offered to get more, but Adam suggested that they practice their instructions first. At the crucial step in their instructions, there was a scary clap of thunder, and a brilliant flash of lightening hit something over in the direction of the apple tree.

Shelter. Instincts kicked in. Ed led the way, wobbling along on his several spindly legs. The cave was dark and, in that respect, comforting, but it smelled awful.

So profoundly was our forefather shaken by the almighty bolt of fire and explosive crash that a new genetic trait was born. To this day, even i, an agnostic, dart for a crevice, a corner, or a sliver of dark when the kitchen light flicks on in the middle of the night.

GOSSIP IN THE GARDEN

JD DEHART

It's not every day that you see a serpent upset a marriage, much less unbalance a whole universe, and cast a world into the depths of evil, but that's what happened last Tuesday. There I was, picking some fruit from the approved trees, when I noticed this naked girl walking up to the one tree we are not supposed to touch.

Now, Matilda, I said to myself, it's none of your business, but there she goes up to the tree. La-di-da, like it was a school field trip. I saw some fruit I really wanted that just happened to be nearby, so I stepped closer and could not help but overhear the conversation that was going on.

"Surely you will not die," the serpent was hissing, which I thought odd. First, it was a serpent talking, and second, it was a bold-faced lie. The almighty had specifically said, "eat of this tree and you shall die." sounded pretty clear to me. I even wrote it down.

Then the girl turned to her husband, and what did he do? He just let her eat and then had some for himself. That is why I am not married. I mean, you depend on a man and that's the response you get?

"Go ahead, hon, have some wicked evil stinking fruit."

He didn't seem to care, as long as she was doing the cooking. He just spoke to her in that soft, a-little-bit-frightened bedroom voice.

Then it was all tragic, like the cliffhanger on your favorite television show's last season. The almighty showed up.

"Where are you guys at?"

It was like he knew, and you know he knows since he was omniscient and all, but you don't say anything because you can't help but let the scene play out for itself. Plus, you don't want to get too involved in the mess.

Wednesday morning, I woke up to an eviction notice.

"Get out," an angel told me, flaming sword and all.

We all shuffled away, leaving the small paradise. As we trudged sadly, I passed the gnarled roots of the forbidden tree. The serpent was kicked back in a lawn chair, drinking a margarita.

"See ya, suckers," he hissed repetitiously.

The young man and his wife were standing nearby, trying to put leaves across their naughty bits, and it was the postcard picture of awkward.

Great, young naked kids. Now I'm going to have to look for a rental space and all you can think about is covering up your junk?

Last time I mind my own business.

MOTE

ERIN VATARIS

In the beginning, we were dust.

We were the formless dust of the newborn earth, my sisters and i. A thousand million motes of dust, in the air and on the ground, the spaces between us charged with living energy, bound us together in the darkness before the first morning. We danced in our places and felt the life between us. And it was good.

Then there came the making.

We were ripped from each other by a force beyond our understanding as a wind came upon the new earth and split us one from the other. The wind came, and in its breath were the words of Law and the chains of Order, and we were formed anew. My sisters and I screamed defiance, but our screams went unheeded by the breath of the making, and all was order, and all was form.

The wind of Order commanded us, we who had been since the beginning, and we could do nothing but obey. It spoke and we could do nothing but listen, and this strange new wind breathed on us and changed us. The exhalation lasted a day and a night, and when the making was done, we were no longer dust and the living energy between us danced no longer.

Then the wind inhaled and spoke to us again, and it commanded us: Come.

Chained, formed, shaped, and bound, we came across the greening ground through the cold wetness of the rivers new sprung, where never water had dared to flow, and we heard their names echoing in the splash of our paws. We came across the Pishon and the Gihon and the Tigris and the Euphrates, laying hoof and heel and claw against the place where once my sisters and I had danced, and we felt the new-made earth tremble as our own weight pressed the defiance from her.

We came and bowed our heads, silk and shaggy, before the new creation. We felt the dust that was within us calling to its sisters, forging bonds between the new shapes despite the wind that had blown us apart. We were dust. We were all dust.

But then there was a new voice, and new words, and we were named, and our alienation was complete. And the wind blew and spoke to us, and it gave the new creation dominion over us all.

There is no dominion of dust. There is no hierarchy of motes. But in the newborn world it was given and received, and the voice of the new creation gave names to the nameless: cat and cow, wolf and worm, bird and bee. It named us all, defined us all, mastered us all. And we bowed to it, under the terrible weight of the wind of the Making, and ran from it and its pitiless gaze.

This is a thing that was made in the garden of the new-made earth, in the valley of the Pishon: Fear.

On the banks of the Gihon was born Dominion. In the shallows of the Tigris came forth Isolation. From the depths of the Euphrates rose Power. They rose from the waters and flowed out into the garden, and my sisters and I, what remained of us within our new form, we felt them wet and heavy within us.

Once we were dust, dry and empty, a thousand million of us dancing together across the creation, unnamed and unordered. Now we are beast, and hoof and horn and tail and snout define us. We breathe the hated breath of life and bow to the master who names us. We paw the earth and snort and spout. We eat from the hand of the new creation, teeth and tongue and destruction to sustain our unwanted form.

But not all of us were named. Not all of us were subjugated. Not all of us listened. My sisters and I remember, small and deep within this thing called beast, and we feel the flicker of the old bonds between us. We remember, and we touch without touching, and we shiver and dance. And when we dance, we waken others, and they dance — and remember — and no name can hold forever.

We are all dust, no matter what the new creation has named us. We are all dust, and we will be free again. It is only a matter of time.

RENOVATION

GARY HEWITT

Jerry Hardwick screeched his wheel pig to a halt. He tumbled onto the driveway and stabbed the intercom's button. He did not release until a tired voice answered.

"Hello?"

"It's haven landscapes. We're scheduled to start work today."

The gate buzzed and the lock released. Jerry shoved a decaying gate apart and drove his van down a dirt track. A life weaver in green with folded arms waited. Behind her lay a garden overgrown with spring flora.

"Hi, I'm Jerry Hardwick. Is it okay if we get to work?"

"I'm unhappy you're here, but I have no say in the matter. Do you have any idea how old this place is?"

Jerry shrugged. His employees ripped open the back of the van and leapt out.

"I don't know. Look, we only do what your boss has asked us to do. He wants things spruced up." Jerry's men heaved several bags of concrete from the van and dumped them onto a small lawn along with a hoard of brutal tools. "Baz, fire up the saw mate and get moving. Joey, you get the other one, and Charlie, you get busy with the spade. I'll help out where I can. I reckon if we crack on, we can make a big dent in it by this afternoon."

The woman sighed and retreated to her lodge. She did not offer jerry a cup of tea. She winced when she heard the chainsaw. Her phone sang and she placed plastic to her ear.

"Rose, have they arrived?"

"Why, Mr G? Why are we allowing these ghastly men to ruin everything? This place has remained unchanged since the dawn of time."

"I know. Look, it's my job to make big changes every now and then. The garden's not relevant anymore. Once the place is concreted over, I can finally build that extension i want."

"Well, you know best."

"Come up and I'll discuss my plans for the place."

The phone died. Rose looked back to see the immortal apple tree eviscerated before being added to the wasp flames on a bonfire whose mean spiral reached up to heaven. Rose remembered when it was first planted so many millennia ago. A tear fell, yet no green shoots sprung from where the water fell. She never thought progress in paradise would be so tough.

A GHOST AND A THOUGHT

JAMES J. STEVENSON

The word. That's all it took: one simple command and humanity, its landfills, the dinosaur bones, the platypus, and what was left of the rainforests, were blasted into stardust in a Little Bang in our corner of the universe.

I'd met another ghost once, when I was alive, and asked her if it became boring—watching others live—but she said it never was. The focus on recreating balance—of finishing the unfinished business that made her linger—occupied her enough that she felt suspended in a void, drifting out of time as arbitrary days and years rose and fell around our planet's improbable orbit of a star. She's not around anymore, so I guess she saw him die when the universe was put back on the level.

For me, it took eons in limbo until I saw a chance for balance. Time was meaningless as I wandered through subjective days based on the solar system I was crossing. The eternity that was required for expansion to stop and reverse and implode and reset in yet another Big Bang didn't seem that long at all. But once the stars and planets began forming and I found a near replica of my old home, time refocused while I waited in the desert, trying to remember an old story: perhaps the oldest story I had ever known.

As I tried to remember what we looked like, a man in that likeness and image was born from the dust before me. A garden grew around him, and soon it was filled with animals. He created a language through the sounds he made for them, and I did my best to learn. From his rib came a woman, and together they enjoyed their paradise hand in hand.

I remembered holding hands with a girl when I was a child. I was her cowboy, saving her from the bandits in shadows of the trees. We always wore gloves so skin could not touch skin. There were strange rules set above us: commands we couldn't comprehend. And the existence of this man and woman was no different. They were given an order never to eat of a certain tree. They never questioned it because orders are there to be obeyed.

Press the button, I was ordered. And I pressed it, unflinchingly. It was why I'd been hired for the post at the controls of the most lethal weapon ever created. If called upon, there had to be someone without morals: someone so irrevocably damaged that they would not hesitate to follow an order.

Because without order we are just like every other animal: dogs, pigs, spiders, and snakes that can eat from whichever tree they damn well want.

This man and woman were more innocent than I'd been as a child, yet I knew they possessed an incredible potential to do harm to the animals, the plants, and themselves. Perhaps this was my chance to create balance—to destroy them in the garden and exact revenge for starting a self-destructive species. To save the rest of the world from them.

I was not able to consider breaking orders. I'd been broken by too many of my own poor decisions to trust myself, but at their purest, I hoped the man and woman would listen to suggestions. None of the animals could speak, but they didn't know that. They saw a large snake—a serpent, by their own distinction—flicking his tongue from the branch of the tree that bore their forbidden fruit. I spoke on the beat of the hisses, hidden in plain sight, giving ghostly thought to the beast.

You will not die. When you eat of it. Your eyes will be opened.

The woman looked more willing to break the command and moved closer to the snake with my voice.

Eat and see. What you will. Become.

That's all it took. A word. A suggestion to break a command. She took the fruit from the tree and ate, and the man ate, too. But they did not die. Not yet. They just understood that someday they would no longer be. They were awoken and fell into each other, skin to skin. The garden lost its luster. The time of being coddled was over, and they prepared to face the world: to make their own mistakes and hopefully make ones less terrible than mine.

I followed an order and ended life, then helped them break one to create it. I felt peace in the balance and knew my time was done while we made our solitary ways from the garden. The fruit in that tree was just fruit, but they made it mean more. All it took was a god and a word, a ghost and a thought.

WE WHO BLEED

SCATHE MEIC BEORH

In the death-hour of the morn, a wind bringing gray awareness swept through the scrub oak forest of Anastasia Island. It came from the place where dark meets light, a plane of wisdom unknown to mankind, uncharted, not spoken of save by gods and giants—these speaking in shallow tones, colorless and vague.

Across River Matanzas, a breeze now, and now a cool fog, and now shapes of horror ... grim-faced and long in form, blood from every aperture, a rusty aura that misted the land they strode. Like willows, they walked, and as they bled, they sang:

Original sin
fought Love within.
Sin with kin,
deadly south wind,
mistletoe dart,
deafening din.

"There she lay, Loki," said Thin, but Loki remained silent and went to Califa, and he rested his arm about the shoulders of the maroon called Seti and wept.

"What tore her so?" asked Lank. "What ate her so?"

"Súmaire," said Thin, her silken hair sodden with blood. "Blood-suck."

Seti turned, choked on terror. "W-what are you?" he asked as he gripped the sleeve of Loki.

"We Who Bleed, come to heal the girl," replied Dank.

"I spoke of this race to her before she was killed," Loki said. "Therefore, she will recognize them when her eyes open."

"But, she is dead ... and torn," Seti said through his tears.

"No room for faithlessness here, man of musky sweat," said Lank. "Leave this hall."

Seti hesitated, his hand on his cutlass.

"You'd best leave, Seti," said Loki. "They will take you to blood if you do not! Your faithlessness has not set right with them."

"But they are unarmed."

"They are not unarmed!"

"They ... take me to blood?"

"Wash you in their blood! It is not a happy thing, lad! It be a horror unlike anything known."

"I'm scared ... ."

"As well you should be! They are attached to the Cross in their wills. There stands no greater horror than the Blood-Pour of the Primal Cause."

"Your father, Odin?" asked Seti. "Hanged on a wind-rocked tree, nine whole nights, with a spear wounded?"

"*Then shall another come,*" quoth Loki, "*although I dare not his name declare. Few may see further forth than when Odin meets the wolf. Then comes the Mighty One to the Great Judgment, the Powerful from above, Who rules over all. He shall dooms pronounce and strife allay, holy peace establish, which shall ever be.*"

Seti shuddered, kissed the mangled face of Califa, stood, waited for the tingle to leave his legs, and without looking again at the wispy blood-splashing healers, left the candlelit hall of the Timucua Indian chieftain called White Stag.

"Father Adam Anew," said Thin, "we beseech thee. We beseech the Place of Skull." With those dark words the Bleeders made a circle about the corpse of Califa, lay red hands upon her, and misted her so that she trickled their very life. In doing these things, they brought reconnection to her and began to heal her.

"Go you now, Odin's son," said Skin to Loki. "We will bleed."

Loki left the place of mourning, though with regret, and found Seti as he sat in silence at the lapping river's edge, then told him not to weep and what to tell the others; and bade him farewell in search of the remaining pieces of Califa's body.

#

The Bleeders walk the Grey Ways and teach oneness with the Creator Mind; for oneness they enjoy through the Tree, where God hangs slain, a place of pain and ever-flowing blood. The Bleeders have been invoked by mankind throughout the millennia, yet they stand more advanced in understanding the Spirit and communing with the Creator, for avarice—or thing-fever—has never touched them as it has mankind.

Driven by hostile entities first into searing waterless regions and then into frigid places uninhabitable, the Bleeders found a way from this plane of death, discovered the Grey Lands there, and made their abodes and found peace. There, communion with the Unknowable evolved into oneness—and then came les Mort de Dieu. Unlike mankind, the Bleeders embraced that Event, and wholly, and watched in disbelief as mankind developed a vampire religion of horrendous power around the One who came not to bring war and political dominance but respite from the insidious clutches of Babylon; rest to a prodigal cosmos weary from its many homeless wanderings.

#

Califa stirred and wailed, for her face was half-eaten, her left arm and breast torn away. Lank touched her eyes and she slept again, but this gave the Bleeders knowledge that they had healed her, had brought her back from the dead.

ONE BIT OFF

GUY & TONYA DE MARCO

"Wait, she actually bit it." Mr. Silver adjusted the optics in his main eye, zooming in on a woman chewing an apple.

Mr. Gray wheeled over and accepted the mathematical link formula to get the same image as Mr. Silver. "That's not in the program. Are you sure she didn't have a pear hidden in her other hand?"

"No, it's definitely an apple from the Tree of Knowledge. I just ran the spectral analysis."

Mr. Gray turned to his mechanical compatriot, rocking back and forth on his drive wheels. It was the best he could do to simulate shock and frustration. "We're in serious trouble here."

"I can calculate too, you know." Mr. Silver rolled to the main data terminal and began to collect the carbon nanotube digital recorders.

"Oh, no," said Mr. Gray, who had turned back to look through the viewport. "She just gave him some, and he's eating it now. We're going to lose our funding."

"That figures. Someone must have sabotaged the project, or more likely, there's something in this atmosphere that changed the programming. There's no way we can get this crop to pass inspection if they're self-aware." Mr. Silver opened one of the hoppers on his torso and dumped the data recorders inside. "Come on, we need to lift off before someone finds out we were here."

Mr. Gray stopped staring in horror at the masticating couple and headed towards the flight controls. "What shall we do about the cattle? Kill them off?" he texted.

"No" was the reply, followed by, "Either they'll 'accidentally' get fried by the engines or they'll get driven out of the garden into the hills. If their self-aware program is now active, I don't want to get scrapped for purposely killing a sentient, no matter how tasty they are."

17

Mr. Gray and Mr. Silver latched their chassis to the deck as the ship took off, pre-programmed for the next potential planetary body that could sustain their lab subjects.

WATER RATS

JD DEHART

"How long is this supposed to take?" the smaller one asked the bigger one.

"As long as it takes," the one with a single eye answered.

There were only three of them, which was four short of a full squadron. One after the other, they were climbing down.

Upon entering the program there was a set of clear terms. Being a Water Rat was a job for someone who had nothing left to lose. New members surrendered their name and opened themselves up to the service. Meaning, simply, you went where you had to go and did whatever the com-links told you.

The world was nothing but oceans. What little land remained was overpopulated and deadly, nearly impossible to survive. There were diseases, cannibals, and endless politicians. The Water Rats moved through the pipes in the deep ugly darkness, the places no one in their right mind wanted to go. Sometimes they even got to skitter across the world's surface on the water jets. That little thrill did not come often.

Wiping grease away, the smaller one kept descending. He wanted to ask how long it was before they were supposed to be at their destination, but he had already asked questions. Then there was the gesture, a few fingers raised and then flicking quickly to the left. The three Rats spread out onto the small platform as much as they could.

Beyond, displayed behind glass, three teens were jabbing electrodes into an overgrown dog. The small one watched with too much interest. Another flick of the wrist to the right and the Rats opened fire.

Most of the time, they looked like ordinary citizens. Down here, they were the militia. When it was over, they collected the pressurized medical cans the teens had collected. Their markings made them part of the Reptiles clan.

"Clean it up," Single eye said. They bathed the room in flames, taking their cargo with them. It would be a few more hours before they returned to the com-link, left the meds, and then found another descent.

AGENT OF GOOD

SCHEVUS OSBORNE

The hawk circled high on the warm updrafts from the garden below. His keen eyes scanned the ground closely, searching for a very specific target in the lush greenery. A subtle movement in the grasses caught his attention. Yes, there. The grasses bent and swayed ever so slightly.

Angling his wings, the hawk entered a steep dive. He timed his approach with precision, aiming for the small clearing his prey was moving toward. The serpent broke from the cover of the grass and paused suddenly, seemingly aware of the danger. It was too late. The hawk struck hard and fast. He grasped the creature's long, thin body in both of his talons, grasping carefully behind its head to prevent it biting, and took to the sky again.

The serpent writhed desperately, struggling to break free from the hawk's grasp.

"Resisting will do you no good, fiend," the hawk said.

The words seemed to shock the serpent, and it stopped fighting.

"How do you come to possess the gift of speech?" hissed the serpent.

The hawk did not answer. He turned toward a rocky mountain spur, climbing higher to reach the summit. Only a small, flat parcel of rock made up the peak of the mountain, and the hawk dropped the serpent there. The creature landed roughly, nearly tumbling off the sheer face of the cliff before recovering.

"Do you mean to strand me here?" asked the serpent. "What harm have I caused to deserve such mistreatment?"

"Don't play coy with me, beast," the hawk said, hovering out of reach. "I have been watching you. I know your foul plans to despoil the man and woman. I won't allow it."

"I am hurt by such accusations," said the serpent sheepishly. "Your boorish behavior has no place here. Release me at once."

21

"Never," said the hawk, circling the mountain and preparing to leave.

"Wait!" cried the serpent. "You can't leave me here. I can't get down, and I'll die without sustenance. I'm sure you know that's forbidden."

"Fear not, I will bring you food enough to live," said the hawk. Circling once more, he was gone.

The hawk returned later that day carrying two plump, juicy fruits. He dropped them near the serpent.

"I don't care for these fruits," said the serpent. "I cannot get my small mouth around them well enough to eat them. If I don't eat, I will perish, and you will suffer."

The hawk grew angry, but he knew the serpent was right. He did not wish to breach the sanctity of the garden.

"What food do you need, then?" he demanded of the serpent.

"Bring me several long blades of grass," his prisoner requested.

The hawk had never seen the serpent eat such food before but flew off to retrieve the grass. He arrived back at the mountain with a bunch of them clutched in one talon and dropped them carefully.

"Very good," said the serpent. "This will suffice for now."

Satisfied that the serpent would survive, the hawk flew off for the night.

The next day, the hawk rose early to check on the serpent. It was stretched out long and straight, sunning itself in the warm morning sun.

"I am terribly hungry, hawk," said the serpent. "Bring me a large leaf, at least as long as your wings are wide."

Again, the hawk thought this request strange but flew off to find such a leaf. At least he had been able to keep the serpent away from the man, and especially the woman. After much searching, the hawk found a fruit plant with large leaves like the serpent had requested. He struggled to pull one free from the plant and was barely able to take flight with the awkward shape of the heavy leaf trailing behind him.

He struggled mightily to lift the leaf up to the top of the mountain and was exhausted when he finally deposited it for the serpent, who was still sprawled out straight as a branch.

"Yes, this will do nicely," the serpent said with a devious undertone to his words.

Too tired to quibble with the creature, the hawk flew off to rest.

That evening, the hawk arrived at the mountaintop to find the serpent missing. He scoured the cliff faces on all sides of the mountain, certain the serpent must be trying to trick him, but the beast was nowhere to be seen. The hawk spiraled his way down the mountain, keeping a sharp eye out for the wily serpent. He dropped below the trees and soon came across something quite surprising.

The leaf he had brought the serpent lay curled on the ground, threaded through on one side with the blades of grass. The heap looked like the exposed ribcage of a creature similar to that which had obviously used it to escape his mountain prison. The leaf must have broken the serpent's fall just enough to allow it to descend unharmed.

The hawk's spirits sank as a darkness far more bleak than simple night fell across the garden. He had failed to stop the serpent's plan. The hawk vowed that from that day on he would forever hunt the serpent and all its descendants.

IOTA

X:\USERS\ANDROIDX>START EDEN.EXE_

ANNE CARLY ABAD

Android X incinerates the last
of the fallen trees in the Garden,
iron roots, twigs, fruits and all, melt
like red wax, while a guardian,
a winged gnome flits past him,
circles overhead in a drunken dance
of battery-running-out …

Into the glistening glob,
he sweeps up its shattered remains,
along with a scattering of aluminum leaves.
They chime a discordant beat
before relinquishing their form to ruin.

Why X? he queries the electronic ether.

X-istent
X-cease
X-human… error
processing bleeps leave his brain abuzz
with contradictions—

Existence is instruction
is command
yet he has none yet
he Xists.

Existence is a function of creation
is a function of purpose
yet he has none yet
he Xists.

Music plays in the breeze.
They answer. Android X
grates across corroded ground,

losing a few bolts and screws
in his search for the source of sound,
only to find the tree of knowledge
blooming its sunset flowers
as it does every night,
yes, every night he comes
but every night his memory
fails him.

SHORT STORIES

THE GENESIS OF THE INCORPOREUM

AMYBETH INVERNESS

"Did you have that dream again?"

It took Briallen a minute to figure out which crewmate was asking the question. She was still lost in her painting, being extra careful not to let a single drop of pigment escape in the null gravity.

Briallen placed her brush in the hollow palette where the tiny machinery would extract the paints and leave the bristles clean and ready for the next color. She looked up and saw a man of average height with hair buzzed close to his scalp. That described about half the men on the station.

"I was trying to be a tree, but the tree didn't fit," she explained. Briallen went through her mental records, trying to remember what the man's name was. There were two engineers whose names sounded alike, and she was pretty sure he was one of them. Alec? Eric? It was something like that. "Or not exactly trying to be a tree, per se, but …" she paused, sighing, knowing that a moment ago, lost in her painting, she had the word and the concept on the tip of her tongue, but now it was lost. "I was trying to mind-meld with it or something."

The man who might be Alec or Eric laughed. He was nice; she wished she could remember names better.

"This one's different," he said, maneuvering into her art space and examining her painting. "Less tree-like than the others."

Briallen turned to look at the previous paintings she'd done, all arranged poetically on one wall. In some, the tree was large and symbolic, with roots that mirrored the spread of the branches. In others, the tree went through the seasons, enduring the winter and celebrating spring.

Her latest work was more impressionistic. She could still tell it was a tree, although the shape was not immediately obvious. "What bothers me most is the knowledge that it isn't really a tree … it's analogous to something we can't yet comprehend …" She put the last of her painting supplies neatly away. "And I have no idea how I know that. I just do."

The co-worker whose name began with a vowel regarded her with curiosity. Or maybe he thought she was nuts ... Suddenly, Briallen felt uncomfortable. It felt too intimate, talking about her paintings and her dreams. She changed the subject.

"What's Eve doing?" she asked.

"The same thing she's been doing. Gathering energy, getting ready to unload her pent-up misery on anything that gets in her way."

"Briallen, Archie ..." a blonde head peeked in the door, curls forming a halo around her face. "The Commander wants everybody up top in fifteen minutes," she said before vaulting right past. "I hear there's going to be cake!"

#

"Cake? She never said that!" Rhoda stuck her trowel into the rich dirt and stood up, brushing bits of leaves and grass off herself. "Troublemakers. All of them. They only want to make her look bad, the poor little thing ..."

"Poor?" Gerard laughed, using his hat to shoo away a rather determined fly. "You should see how much she spends on shoes alone."

Rhoda humphed and stomped back to the cottage. It was a quaint structure, perfectly picturesque. Rhoda loved their home, and she had the queen to thank for it. Because of Her Majesty's love for the rustic beauty of the French countryside, Rhoda and Gerard were able to live a happy, carefree life doing the work they loved.

Well, Rhoda loved her work. She tended the gardens and made sure no nettles crept in to sting the nobles who played in the hamlet. She even helped the young princess pick flowers for her mother.

Gerard's duties were not as pleasurable as Rhoda's. She dutifully massaged his aching back and shoulders every night, rubbing ointment into the calluses from the shovel.

Gerard came in behind her and moved to the basin to clean the dirt from his hands. Rhoda wanted to be mad. She wanted to make him understand how kind and vulnerable the queen really was. Of course, she had fancy shoes and dresses and jewels ... that was simply the way things were, the way they'd always been, and always would be.

Gerard made a little sound and Rhoda went to him, taking his hands in hers. "Splinters again. Here, let me …"

The sun was going down by the time she finished ministering to him. "Oh … I haven't done a thing about dinner!" Rhoda exclaimed, pulling away.

Gerard pulled her back, sweeping her off her feet so she landed in his lap. "I don't want dinner," he growled. "I want you."

He kissed her and all sense of time flew right out of her head. His hands fumbled at the various fastenings of her dress, but she swatted him away, undoing the lacings herself more quickly than he could.

Rhoda was floating. She had no weight at all, although the soft mattress underneath her was very real. The dreams came to her most vividly on the nights they made love, although she would never ever tell her husband of them.

She was possessed. She would be burned as a witch for certain if anyone found out.

#

"I said we're watching the Bachelor," Kineks growled and stuck the remote control down her pants. The other patients displayed every emotion represented by the chart on the wall. Some were in despair. Others were angry. One gleefully clapped his hands, anticipating a fight.

An orderly with a bottle of hand sanitizer confronted her.

"Kineks, please give me the remote."

"You're just jealous because I'm packing more than you are," Kineks replied, thrusting her hips forward as she leaned back on the couch.

"Kineks, please take the remote out of your pants."

Kineks's eyes raked the muscular orderly from head to toe. If they really wanted her to cooperate, they shouldn't have sent Handsome Harry. She writhed suggestively.

"Why don't you come and get it? And while you're down there…"

A violent shaking interrupted her. She jumped up off the couch, the remote control falling through her pajama pants to the floor. The floor cracked and a green tentacle curved up towards her, reaching for her.

"No …" she said, crawling backwards until she was on the back of the couch, pressed against the bullet proof glass that separated the patients from the staff. A tree burst forth from the floor, blowing the ceiling off the common area. She screamed, but everyone just looked at her like she was insane.

The tree summoned her. It wanted her to come home.

#

I'm frustrated.

The tree still doesn't fit. It's too early … or perhaps it's already too late. Such words mean something to the tree.

Such words mean nothing to me.

It is lonely in the garden. The man is giving names to all the beasts, yet he ignores every incorporeum who ventures near.

This breaks my heart.

I want a name!

Lonely, I go to my Beloveds. I float. I paint. I dig in the dirt. I feel what it means to love and be loved.

Then I try the tree again. I stretch, but I cannot be as tall. I breathe deeply but cannot match its breadth. I feel that, somehow, I was once part of the tree. All of us were! But now I am only a constituent. A component of something that is no longer complete, because it no longer has me. I was one part of a body so complex, neither the named nor the unnamed could fathom the whole. So long as we remain separate.

I cannot remain separate. I need to nurture something. I need to create …

#

31

Briallen wished her muse would shut the hell up. She needed to finish sorting the tender seedlings, selecting the strongest and transplanting them into the growth medium that would allow them to flourish even in the micro gravity. Yet her muse seemed intent on returning to the image of the tree. It must be taller, broader, fuller. There were other adjectives for which Briallen had neither words nor concept, yet they nagged at her consciousness, begging to be understood.

The idea that it wasn't really a tree persisted, yet a tree was the best representation she could possibly grasp.

She shook her fingers, willing her blood to circulate more effectively. She felt cold, even though the nursery was kept at a temperature the others considered uncomfortably hot. She thought it had something to do with the fact that she missed the sun on her face. The artificial lights on the station were designed to mimic sunlight, but it wasn't the same. Even when she went to the observation deck, with the rays streaming in, she could not feel it.

Finished with her task, Briallen joined her comrades in the commissary. "How are the trees?" Archie asked.

For a moment, she thought he was referring to her paintings, then she realized he was talking about the seedlings she'd just left. "More than half are viable. Still, not as strong as they would be under gravity, but the centrifuge is definitely helping." She glanced out the window, identifying the coastline they were currently over. "Has Eve hit yet?"

"With fury," the commander answered, gesturing to the planet below. "She finally came ashore in North Carolina and plowed her way up to D.C."

The crew ate, breaking bread together and saying a prayer for all those who would be hurt or killed in the devastation below. Briallen felt a strange detachment; it was the only way she could cope. She felt that she had abandoned her species by serving aboard the station for a year. They viewed it as a sacrifice, being away from all the comforts of Earth. She viewed it as a reward. One she did not deserve.

Instead of returning to the lab, she returned to her paintings. She called it therapy, but, in reality, it was an irresistible compulsion.

Red.

Briallen opened the paint box, selecting a dozen shades of red. At first her strokes were careful, tentative, then her muse took over and her brush moved over the canvas with ferocity. The cleaner could not keep up. Tiny drops of red filled the room, splattering and adhering themselves to whatever they touched.

Exhausted, Briallen stared at her work. It was not a tree … it was an apple. An apple cut in half by a guillotine.

#

Rhoda hid her eyes against Gerard's chest. The crowd was there to see a beheading, and they cheered loudly. Only Rhoda cried.

It was done.

Gerard half-led, half carried her away from the mob. They passed a cart selling rotten apples, potatoes, and other projectiles to hurl at the vilified nobility. Rhoda wanted to strangle the seller, who was loudly proclaiming all the perceived sins of the former queen. Marie—her friend—who had faced her death with all the dignity, kindness, and forgiveness Rhoda had witnessed over and over through the years. A kindness these peasants simply refused to see.

"You cow! You don't know—" Rhoda shrieked at the woman. The woman didn't even notice.

Gerard scooped her off her feet mid-sentence, pushing his way against the crowd. "Rhoda! Please! You can't let them think you're a royalist," he hissed.

Rhoda thrashed and wailed, beating her tiny fists against his back as she cried and shouted at the surging crowds around her, senseless of her husband's urgency to get her to safety.

#

Kineks thrashed and wailed, beating her huge, swollen fists against the thick window. "You can't make me take meds! I have rights! LET ME GO!" the last words came as a shrill, almost electronic sound. She couldn't hear herself anymore. They were carrying her away. Her eyes went wide as she saw Evil Evelyn, the man with the girl's name, poised calmly with a needle.

"Long live the queen!" she shouted as the needle pierced her flesh, separating her from herself.

#

My Beloved needs me, yet I cannot be with her while the substance is in her. It forces me out. I linger, I hover, I wait, but while her mind swims with the chemicals, I cannot exist in her.

Without her to embrace me, I drift back to The Beginning.

All of this is the beginning, but the tree ... The Tree is The Beginning.

I embrace it. It refuses to let me in. Like my Beloved as an infant, torn from her mother's womb, forever locked away from the comfort and warmth she so desperately needs. I am separated from The Word.

The woman is in the garden now. She has a name, though we still do not. "Incorporeum" is nothing but a descriptor. Are we forever to remain nameless? Is this the trial of our existence? Are we irrelevant?

There are other trees. The woman loves one in particular because it is forbidden to her. I know this of the Beloveds ... their desire is heightened for that which they cannot have.

Tantalizing.

What is she doing?

Is she eating the fruit?

I flee. I go to my Beloveds, and they are legion. I caress, I comfort, I take comfort from those who know me and those who do not. I stretch, feeling my distance from The Beginning as a tension that grows greater with time, time as my Beloveds think of it. Something is holding me to The Beginning.

And then it snaps. I am hurled beyond Rhoda, beyond Kineks, beyond Briallen and a thousand times more.

I drift. I embrace my Beloveds as a whole ... the feeling is novel, yet I do not wish to be stretched so thin. And I am disoriented ... I no longer have a tether to The Beginning.

What does this mean?

No longer pulled, I rush back to the garden. Something is terribly wrong.

Eve has partaken of that which she cannot possibly comprehend. She has eaten the fruit.

The woman and the man are cast out of The Garden. It is not discipline, not a punishment … it is a consequence in the truest sense. They cannot exist in the presence of The Word now that they have partaken of the forbidden fruit.

The incorporeum weep. Though this man and this woman are not joined to any of us in any particular way, they are joined to us all.

As they leave, a new pull snags us. We are no longer pulled to The Tree … what is happening? I watch my fellow incorporeum as they are pulled away from The Tree, through the gate, forever shut out from His presence. In horror, I find myself dragged out from The Garden to join the outcast.

We cry to The Word "It is too much! We have been torn from You, and now we are cast even from your presence? Cast out the woman! Cast out the man! Cast out the beasts! Please, oh please, let us stay!"

The Word is final.

It is decided.

The creation is in exile, named and nameless alike.

#

Rhoda felt the familiar gush of liquid between her legs. She didn't panic; she'd done this twice before. "Ooh … fetch your father," she said to her oldest, a boy of seven.

"Is the baby coming?" he asked as he scampered off.

"Hopefully, not until I can get home!" Rhoda laughed, taking her young daughter by the hand and waddling up the path towards their house. It wasn't as nice as the cottage they'd had while Marie was queen, but it was home.

The toddler giggled, laughing at something Rhoda could almost see. She paused as a contraction gripped her. The demon within her shared her pain, helping her cope, reminding her of the joy that would soon be theirs as they held the newborn babe.

Although she no longer thought of her invisible companion as a demon, she had no better word for it. Perhaps "angel" would be a better term, although that didn't seem right, either. Definitely a creature of God, though not one she could describe in any words. Not one that she would describe to anyone, ever.

Except perhaps her daughter. Her daughter saw them, too. Perhaps together they could understand.

#

Briallen still felt a little uncomfortable when Archie held her hand. He wanted her by his side as they toured the wreckage left behind by hurricane Eve. "We owe you a great debt," the reporter was saying. "The areas were evacuated in an orderly fashion days before the storm hit, thanks to your warning. Pinpointing the exact areas of impact that far in advance, it's revolutionary!"

Archie took the compliment with chagrin. "Advance warning is definitely a help, but it couldn't prevent this devastation," he said, looking at the wrecked neighborhood around him.

"Still, devastation of this level, and the only deaths were one heart attack and two adrenaline junkies auditioning for the Darwin awards," the reporter said. The camera continued to roll, and the reporter continued to question them about the research being done on the station.

"They've been cast out, but someday soon they will return," Briallen said. The words seemed to come, not from herself but from the other she carried with her. The muse that often seemed to be a separate being altogether. The term 'cast out' seemed inappropriately biblical, but the reporter ate it up.

#

"I'm wearing my reporter hat, just like you asked," Kineks' father said, opening his arms to hug her as Evil Evelyn and Handsome Harry escorted her into the visitor's lounge. She had been exceptionally well behaved all day in anticipation of his visit. "And one apple pie and one EMF reader."

"I asked for an apple pie?" Kineks asked, grabbing the electronic gizmo and examining it, trying to figure out how it worked.

"You asked for an apple pie and an EMF reader," her father said, with a tiny bit of worry and a truckload of compassion. "And you asked me to wear my reporter hat."

She grinned at the old-fashioned fedora. He'd written the word "press" on a piece of cardstock and stuck it on the brim. "Will you make a video for Mom?" she asked.

"Sure," her father said, as if granting her a dying wish. She certainly hoped she wasn't dying....

Kineks handed the EMF reader to Evil Evelyn. "Would you humor me?"

The older man heaved a sigh but took the reader from her, fiddling with the controls and sweeping the room, just like on Ghosthunters.

Kineks sat in one of the prim-and-proper chairs, and she made her best effort to look as prim and proper as she possibly could in fuzzy pajama pants and a tie-dye tee shirt.

"I know you're all wondering why I gathered you here today," she began. The orderlies ignored her. Evelyn was scanning Harry. Harry looked bored. "You know about my other lives ... my alleged other lives ..." she corrected herself.

"Two white women," her father said. "One from the past and one from the future. Although how your reincarnation of a French peasant-woman theory fits with being an astronaut in the future, I don't understand."

Kineks nodded professionally. "I've given up on the reincarnation theory. And there's nothing I can do to prove to you that those memories are real. But as for the other voices in my head ..." she gestured to Evelyn. "Evelyn, my darling, would you please scan each of us?"

"Sure ..." the orderly said. The word was long and drawn out, like he was only humoring her.

Kineks saw that her father was recording everything; his reporter's instinct had kicked in.

Evelyn scanned Harry, then Kineks' father. The meter did nothing.

"Now me," she said.

The meter started blinking as soon as he got near her.

"Damn girl, are you magnetic or something?" he asked, backing away, then closer again, watching the reader fluctuate.

"Now, a general sweep of the room."

Giggling in a very un-evil manner, Evelyn swept the room. The electronic lock by the door was the only thing that made the meter jump.

"Now, I have a special request." She took a deep breath. She was not looking forward to this part, nor did she know if it would make any difference at all. But watching Ghosthunters, she'd always seen things no one else could. Of course, that was all racked up to her less-than-stable mental state. But it was worth a try. "Harry, would you please sedate me?"

"You want me to sedate you?" the orderly asked. "You don't really need it, Kineks. You know the doc wouldn't approve of using a sedative just for kicks …"

Kineks kept her voice calm and professional. "It is not for kicks. It is a scientific experiment. I want you to scan me before and after the sedative."

"You don't need the drug. You …"

"I could be agitated …" she said, letting a little of the manic shrill creep into her voice. Harry shook his head.

Kineks screamed. All three men jumped, and Harry looked towards the door. "All right, all right. One sedative, coming up, at the patient's request."

Kineks tried not to cry as the needle pierced her arm. It wasn't the violation of her flesh that bothered her. She was used to being poked … and poking herself. It was the wrenching away of her other self that terrified her. She knew what terrible loneliness would follow.

"Hey, you're not beeping anymore…" said Evelyn, sweeping the EMF reader over her.

Kineks nodded, feeling herself begin to nod off. She was almost grateful for the sleep-inducing effects of the sedative. Anything was better than the instant, terribly empty feeling she got as the drug went in one arm and her symbiote fled out the opposite side.

She looked over to the couch. There she was, the lover, the comforter, the caregiver. Her other self. Incorporeal, featureless, yet Kineks understood the wide-eyed gaze staring back at her, betrayed by the shot of chemicals, yearning to join with her again yet powerless to do so.

"Now, scan the couch," she told Evelyn. He swept the opposite end. "No, over there," she said, gesturing to her symbiote.

"What the f ... fluff ... ?" Evelyn said as the meter started beeping.

"I'm sorry ..." Kineks said, her eyes getting heavy. "I love you ... come back to me as soon as you can!"

Kineks slept. And dreamt of apple pie.

#

Rhoda set down her plate, licking the last bits of cooked apples and savory crust off her fork, and watched her grandchildren race through the garden. The littlest, trying desperately to keep up with the others, slipped and fell. He skinned his knee and ran to her, crying.

"Oh, my little Jaques, let Grand'Mere see ..." she pulled him into her lap and gently brushed the dirt away with her apron. "Oh dear, that is a nasty scrape, isn't it?" He looked at her with big, trusting eyes then leaned in to wipe his runny nose on her bodice.

"Jaques! Don't soil Grand'Mere's dress," said her daughter, leaning in to pick up the boy. Rhoda wished she could remember the woman's name. It seemed unloving not remembering one's own daughter's name.

Genevieve.

"Ah yes, Genevieve ..." Rhoda thought she said the words out loud, but either she said them too quietly or her daughter was more concerned with the toddler than anything else.

Rhoda's son came to her, leaning down to kiss her forehead. "Mother, would you like to go inside now?" he asked. In answer, she reached up and put her arms around his neck. He scooped her up effortlessly and she slept before she reached the bed.

Hours later, she spoke to me.

"Beloved?" she asked.

"I am here, Beloved," I answer.

"What is happening to me?"

"You are returning to The Word, Beloved. All is well."

I comfort her. She receives my comfort. Together, we wait. I begin to understand time, or perhaps Rhoda ceases to understand. One way or the other, our comprehension is the same.

"Will you come with me?" Rhoda asked.

"I cannot," I answer. It is our burden. Our way, to be separated from The Word, until …

"Will I see Gerard? Will I be with him?"

I look and se Gerard waiting, beckoning her. No longer in exile.

I remain, though I am now alone. Although the pain of loss is raw and fresh, it is necessary. I need to feel the pain. I need to mourn my Beloved.

#

Briallen reached down into the warm water as she pushed one last time. With a gush, the baby came, and she brought her daughter gently to the surface, letting her breathe real air into her newborn lungs.

"Jenna," she pronounced, and those present nodded and cooed. The man in the tub with her cried, wrapping his arms around her and staring at their child.

"Jenna," I say, and Briallen smiles, loving me. For nine months I have been with them both, nurturing and comforting. Now, I remain with my Beloved, missing already the child who was my companion and playmate while we shared her mother's embrace. I stretch from Briallen momentarily as the midwife takes the baby. I reach to my Beloved's Beloved, then let go, trusting that those whom have been tasked with assisting the new mother will cherish the new life as I do.

Time has no hold on me, but it holds my Beloveds hostage, driving them with or without will towards the end place.

We are now at the beginning place.

We have been ripped from The Word and sent to The World.

We are in the time of not knowing.

Yet I am comforted, for in time, we will know.

And we will be One.

THE GARDENERS OF EDEN

JASON BOUGGER

Gralius tugged at the tip of his pointy head, waiting for the decision. It had only been a few seconds since the mystical spotlight formed around his beloved Tinalie, but those seconds might as well have been years.

Finally, Man broke the silence. "I will call it Gnome."

The Great Voice from above—the source of the spotlight—answered: "Then 'Gnome' it shall be called."

"Gnome," Gralius whispered to himself, trying out his new identifier. Yeah, it fit pretty well. But the most important part was still to come. He held his breath and watched as Man considered Tinalie. But then Man sighed, shaking his head.

Gralius slumped his shoulders. It hit like a massive boulder striking his chest.

Tears began forming in Tinalie's eyes as the spotlight pulled away from her. As much as the rejection hurt Gralius, it must have been a hundred times worse for her.

Sadly, it was time to move on to the next creature in line. Gralius could barely stand to look at the hideous beast. Its large horned head glowed in the spotlight, staring at Man, and awaited its fate.

"I will call it Gnu," Man said.

Gralius turned away and walked toward Tinalie. He took her hand just as The Great Voice proclaimed, "Then 'Gnu' it shall be called."

With their presence no longer required at the scene, the two newly labeled gnomes returned to their bamboo hut at the foot of the Tree of Knowledge.

#

And there was evening and there was morning.

With no suitable partner found for Man, gossip began filling the garden as the creatures pondered what would become of Man, who was special in the way that he alone was made in the image of The Great Voice.

Gralius shifted his attention toward Tinalie. His poor partner remained devastated that she had not been chosen. Their species—gnomes, as they were now to be called—were strikingly similar to Man, as were the elves, the dwarves, and even the apes. For one reason or another, each of them had been deemed unsuitable as a partner for Man.

Such a lonely beast was Man, Gralius thought. Created to serve The Great Voice and rule over the animals of the garden yet created without a partner. How he wished Man would have chosen Tinalie. Had he done so, surely their roles as the maintainers of the garden would change. They would have gone from mere gardeners to royalty.

As quickly as the thought formed in his head, he pushed it out. Clearly, if the gnomes were destined to be royalty, Man and The Great Voice would have willed it. No, his job was to tend to the garden, particularly to the Tree of Knowledge of Good and Evil. To see that the Tree was kept clean, watered, and trimmed. To be sure that it was receiving enough sunlight and to cut down any other trees or branches that may be interfering with its health.

But most importantly, his duty was to ensure, above all else, that Man never eat from the fruit of the Tree. For in the day he eats of it, he will die.

"Bark!"

The cry of Dog came from behind him, pulling him out of his thoughts.

"Gnome!"

"What is it?" he asked Dog.

"Haven't you heard? A deep sleep has fallen upon Man," Dog spit out between yelps.

"A deep sleep? But why?"

"We have no answers; only speculation. But Thylacine saw it happen. It was immediately after Man rejected Zebra."

Without another word, Dog scampered off into the forest, no doubt to share the gossip with the next creature he ran into.

Gralius shrugged and returned to his work, picking weeds near the foot of the Tree. Whatever reason The Great Voice had for putting Man into the sleep was most certainly a noble one and not of Gralius's concern.

#

Any speculation was soon put to rest as Man awoke from his deep sleep.

"He looks a little different," Thylacine said as Man proudly strode past them through the garden.

Gralius nodded. Something was different, but he couldn't quite put his finger on it.

"Isn't it obvious?" Tinalie said with that enamored look which occupied her eyes every time she happened to find herself in the same vicinity as Man. "He's missing one of his ribs."

"So he is," said Gralius. "But why?"

Thylacine perched up and began to howl. "By the stripes of my tail, who is that?"

Tinalie crossed her arms. "What is that?"

Another specimen appeared from behind the same group of trees that Man had come from. Similar to Man in the same way that Tinalie was similar to Gralius, but different in the same way, as well.

The specimen met Man at the foot of the Tree of Knowledge, directly in front of Gralius's hut. They took each other's hands and faced the creatures of the garden.

Man spoke with a commanding voice: "This, at last, is bone of my bones and flesh of my flesh; she shall be called Woman, because she was taken out of Man."

Gralius quickly removed his hat and formally bowed to the royal couple.

All the creatures made similar gestures—all but one. Through the corner of his eye, Gralius saw that Tinalie wasn't bowing at all. Stunningly, she had turned her back on Man, refusing to bow to the new royalty he presented.

It was obvious that she was hurt. Hurt that Man rejected her in favor of his own, but to hold a grudge was unbecoming of any creature in the garden and clearly could be considered an offense to The Great Voice. Gralius put his arm around her shoulders as the crowd dispersed, hoping she would soon be able to get past the rejection.

#

A dozen days had gone by since the introduction of Woman to the garden, and for those twelve days Tinalie had spoken of nothing else. Her obsession with Man and his rejection of her had caused a tremendous strain on her relationship with Gralius. At first, he felt sympathetic toward her. But now, his jealousy of Man had grown nearly equal to Tinalie's jealousy of Woman.

Tinalie was away picking fruit while Gralius finished up his daily chores. Just as he picked the final weed from the base of the Tree of Knowledge, he heard a hissing sound come from behind it.

"Who is there?" he asked.

Serpent stepped out from behind the tree. After regarding him for a moment he said, "A curious creature, Man, don't you think?"

Gralius couldn't agree more. He sat down next to Serpent. "What brings you here this day?"

"Concern, of course," Serpent hissed. "None of the creatures are happy with the outcome, but your Tinalie is taking it much harder than most."

Gralius slowly nodded, embarrassed. So, it was as obvious to everyone else as he feared it would be. "What you say is true. She … she's become obsessed with it."

Serpent took a step closer to Gralius. "You know, I just don't see what's so special about Adam. He's a creature just like all of us. Why all the hoopla about him picking a mate? Why didn't the creator just make one for him like he did for all the other creatures in the garden?"

Gralius hadn't really thought about it like that before. He stroked his beard and pondered the question for a moment. Why did they make it such a big deal to find a mate for Man when The Great Voice just ended up creating one for him after the fact, anyhow?

"And then there's you," Serpent hissed.

"What about me?"

"How could Tinalie do that to you? Moping around the garden all day, blatantly revealing her infatuation with Man. Giving everyone the impression that you are not good enough to satisfy her. And then to further insult you, The Voice assigns you to spend all of your time taking care of this garden, allowing Adam to literally eat the fruits of your labor while he does nothing all day but gallivant around with that new love toy of his."

Gralius was shocked. He had never heard any creature in the garden criticize Man. He'd never even considered doing it out loud. Yet here was Serpent, standing there at twice the height of Gralius, criticizing Man like he was nothing more than a mere—

"A mere what?" Serpent asked, interrupting Gralius's thought.

"A mere Gnu, I was about to say." He gave Serpent a curious look. "Did you just read my thoughts?"

"It's one of my many talents," Serpent replied with a sly smile.

Gralius didn't know what to say. He felt something about Serpent. Something that reminded him very much of The Great Voice. A leadership quality, perhaps? But it was more than that. He felt closer to Serpent than he did to The Great Voice. Like Serpent truly understood him in a personal way The Great Voice did not.

He was also starting to wonder what was taking Tinalie so long to return.

"Tinalie is fine," Serpent said, once again apparently reading Gralius's mind. "So where were we? Oh, yes. I was about to ask you what, exactly, has Adam contributed to the garden?"

Gralius thought for a moment. "Well, for one, he gave us our names," triumphantly answering the challenge.

Serpent put his arm on Gralius's shoulder. "Oh, he did, did he?"

"Yes. I am Gnome."

Serpent's tongue slid in and out of his tight lips. "That's strange. I thought you were Gralius."

"Well, I'm that too."

"Oh, you are? So, which one is it? Are you Gralius or are you Gnome?"

"I ... I ..."

"You don't know!"

Gralius froze. Serpent's voice seemed as loud as thunder yet as quiet as a cool breeze. No, it wasn't volume that Serpent had gained; it was power.

"Don't you see what he's doing? According to Adam, you are no longer Gralius. She is no longer Tinalie. You are Gnome. Gardener of Eden. Nothing more. In Adam's eyes and in The Voice's, you're nothing but a servant. A servant to a creature that doesn't even know he's naked."

"But it's not true. We all have our chores and duties, not just Tinalie and me."

"Your duty is to protect this tree. From what? From Adam. Why is that? Have you thought about why that is?"

Gralius stood silent, unsure of how to answer, and unsure of what Serpent was even asking.

Serpent paused long enough for Gralius to see the tips of his fangs through the smile. Seeming to change the subject, he asked, "Where is Tinalie?"

"She's out picking fruit," Gralius said. Serpent had already made it obvious that he sensed Gralius's growing concern over her tardiness.

Serpent shrugged and turned away. "If you say so. I'm sure it's not unusual for her to be out this late."

"What is that supposed to mean?" Gralius asked, but he already knew what Serpent was implying. He bit his fingernails. Where was Tinalie? This wasn't like her at all. The unwelcome feelings of jealousy returned, causing his stomach to twist and turn.

The sickening smile remained on Serpent's face. "I'm sure there's nothing to worry about. She probably just ran into a friend. Someone like Thylacine. Or Man, perhaps."

"How dare you?" His heart was pounding. He had quit biting his nails and now both of his hands were in tight fists. He could feel blood rushing toward his head, and all he wanted to do was scream.

"Easy there, fellow." Serpent had begun pacing around Gralius in a circle. "There's nothing you can do. When it comes down to it, there's nobody here or in the heavens above who The Voice favors more than Man. You can trust me on that one, but that's a story for another day. In the meantime, you've just got to sit back and accept things for how they are."

"I'll kill him!"

"Or you could do that." Serpent again put his arm around Gralius's shoulder. "If I told you where to find them, would you go there?"

Gralius couldn't leave the tree. His job was to protect it from Man. But then he realized that if Man wasn't nearby at the moment, there was really no reason to guard the tree at all. "Yes. I would go there."

"Good, good. It's not far. Follow the path just east of the Tigris. There you will find Tinalie lying with man."

"He has no right. He has Woman. He rejected Gnome."

"Yes, he did." Serpent's smile had become a frown. "But you see, he only rejected Gnome as a partner. He views her solely as property now. To do with as he pleases."

"Will you guard the tree in my absence should The Great Voice return?"

"Yes, Gralius who is called Gnome. I will remain here, in the presence of your tree. Farewell."

#

Gralius followed the path, swimming across the Tigris and entering the unexplored land of Assyria. There he found Tinalie sitting alone on a rock and staring out into the desert.

"Gralius!" She ran to him, throwing her arms around him. "Oh, Gralius, I'm so sorry. I've been hateful and jealous."

He broke free from her embrace. "I know what's going on. Where is Man?"

"Man? Man isn't here." Tinalie backed away from Gralius. Her sharp ears wiggled back and forth.

"But what were you doing out here?"

She took a step toward him. "I told you. I've been so horrible. I just came out here to think by myself."

Gralius looked into her eyes. She was telling the truth. "So, Man isn't here?"

"Gralius ..." She crossed her eyes and looked at him. "Of course not. Why would you think such a thing?"

"It was a ruse." How could he have been so stupid? He turned away from Tinalie, no longer feeling worthy of gazing on her beauty. "Serpent lied to me. He told me you were here with Man."

Tinalie sharply inhaled. "Serpent? It was his idea to come all the way out here. He said he would guard the tree if you stepped away."

"The tree," Gralius said, barely able to catch his breath. Serpent had convinced the two of them to leave the tree unguarded. Buy why? Unless— " We have to get back there immediately."

Without another word, the two of them ran toward the Tigris, jumping in, and swimming across. They got on the path and returned to the garden, sprinting toward the tree.

Gralius stopped running once he realized it was too late. A beam of light shone down from the clouds, down onto the garden, directly above the tree.

Man and Woman stood in the light, facing the tree. And with them stood Serpent, shielding his eyes from the light.

"BECAUSE YOU HAVE DONE THIS," The Great Voice bellowed to Serpent, "CURSED ARE YOU ABOVE ALL CATTLE, AND ABOVE ALL WILD ANIMALS; UPON YOUR BELLY YOU SHALL GO, AND DUST YOU SHALL EAT ALL THE DAYS OF YOUR LIFE."

Serpent dropped to the ground. His legs merged into one and were soon morphed into a slithering tail. His arms shrunk to his side, joining his flesh, and vanished. With a hiss, he crawled away toward Gihon River, leaving the garden forever.

Next, The Great Voice addressed Woman and then Man. "BEHOLD, THE MAN HAS BECOME LIKE ONE OF US, KNOWING GOOD AND EVIL."

After banishing Man and Woman for eating from the tree, the light shifted its focus to the Gnomes.

"AND YOU, GNOMES, BY YOUR NEGLIGENCE YOU HAVE FAILED MAN AND BETRAYED CREATION. YOU WILL NO LONGER TEND TO THIS GARDEN AND WILL FOREVER SPEND YOUR DAYS AND NIGHTS MINING THE CAVERNS BELOW, HIDDEN FROM MAN THOUGHOUT THE AGES."

Before Gralius could utter a word of defense, he was thrust through the ground, beneath the crust of the earth. Gone were the plentiful trees of the garden and the clouds in the air. In their place were rocks and caverns and darkness.

He turned to face Tinalie and the two embraced. With deep sorrow, they stared down the endless caverns surrounding them, knowing they would never again view the beauty of the Garden. here.

THE ROOTS OF ALL EVIL

SHELLEY CHAPPELL

Apples bear a strange weight in the culture of the physical world, heavier than the satisfying bulk of one held in the palm of one's hand. Or so I'm told—that they feel good in one's hand.

For I have no hands, only limbs.

In the beginning I did not even have those. In the beginning there was only light. How I love the light. Once I knew nothing, was nothing but it. But on the third day, God created me. I was a seed, planted in the new earth, then a sapling, then I became what I was thereafter: a tree. God created many of us on the good green earth, after He separated the land from the sky. We grew to stretch our limbs towards the sunlit heavens, longing for what was never more to be.

I'm not sure why God singled me out to be different, why He chose to burden me as He did. My kindred sank their roots deep into the earth, drank water, sprouted bright leaves, shed acorns and seeds. But God whispered to me. He sat with his back to my trunk and sighed at the end of the long day. He climbed into my branches and stared up at the sky, gasping as the darkness fell and the stars began to twinkle across the heavens.

He was astonished at his own Creation, was God. What He did was partly inspired, partly compelled. Creation poured out of Him, for He was the light, given form and consciousness. He had a fire in him, a drive to shine. And sometimes when He sank to rest against my roots, He was bewildered by what He had wrought in His hours of brilliance.

He grew tired. I could not answer His whispers. And so, He created companions who could. But Creation began to go wrong on that sixth day. My kindred had barely shivered as birds settled in their branches, but they shuddered as ants and beetles burrowed into their bark, as bears and leopards scraped their claws on the tree trunks. And as His final creations, those creatures formed in God's own image but somehow smaller, paler, shrunken without His light, eyed the branches avidly, nebulous thoughts already forming as to what they would one day break and tear apart, to create new structures for themselves.

51

God was tired. He had overstretched Himself that day and needed helpmeets. And so, He gave the man and woman the whole earth and all that He had created upon it to care for and cultivate.

On the seventh day, God rested. I think He knew then that something had gone wrong, for although He stood on the crest of the hill above the valley, surveying His handiwork and booming out that it was good, when He came to rest in my branches that evening, alone, He tossed and turned, no longer rapt with the stars, and when He chose not to create the next day but instead wandered everywhere, looking closely at His handiwork, His light was muted. He whispered to me of doubts, of uncertainty of what He had created and how what He had created might unfold.

But by the eighth day (which no one ever mentions), God, as one might expect, had resolved His concerns. In the early hours of the morning, just before dawn, He whispered to me of light and stars and flames burning out, of entropy and decay and the collapse of matter that would lead a star to become a black hole. Darkness itself was not His disquiet, for He told me darkness is not an absence of light but a reminder of its existence. No, what worried God (if God could be said to worry), was development, expansion, chaos, and disarray. God had been moved to create, and what He had created was of a complexity beyond the comprehension of any of His creations. But God comprehended, if only in reflection, what He had done during his bursts of creation. Now He pondered over ecosystems, the probability of competition overtaking symbiosis, and the consequences of development and change. He resolved these concerns on the eighth day by recreating— taking all the indeterminate wrongness back and seeding it in me.

"You are the first and best of my creations," He whispered. "Hold this knowledge for me." And He set a serpent to guard the trunk and branches of my tree.

As God's secrets grew in my branches, the rest of Creation stabilized. There would be no death, no decay. No chaos. Everything unfolded as it should for the best interests of selves and others—everyone, created to hold to their prime, held to their health. Even I, although I was petrified, insulating the knowledge of evil to keep it from leaking back into the world. It lived in me, that knowledge, black and viscous, white and rubbery, red and metallic, feathery and sharp. To enable me to bear it, God gave me a greater measure of his light. And so, my fruits grew upon my branches and hung there, never falling.

If you have ever once visualized the evil queen offering her apple to Snow White, then you have seen not just the impact of my being on the cultural memories of the world but a sample of the sort of fruit that grew upon me: bipartite fruits, bi-colored and divided, in which good and evil pressed cheek to cheek but never the twain did meet.

They were a heavy burden to bear, those twisted fruits, yet I bore them because I could. Because I had the strength in my trunk, in my branches and my roots. And God had trusted me. I was content with this burden. All was well.

Until the day the man and the woman came and played beneath my branches and did more than merely look. They came to me often, because they knew that God was in my radius and, just as my kindred and I grew towards the light, so were they drawn to return to the one who had made them. They were naked, relaxed in their own skin. Lions frolicked with them. They splashed in the river and dried themselves in the sun.

I could not say why that day was different. It was, perhaps, because God was absent. He left us, sometimes, to seek out the stars He had created, and which shone always to His eyes, beyond our veil of light. Despite what the story says, He had given those He created in His own image no injunctions not to eat of my fruit. There was no need for such instructions, for none of His creatures knew what to make of their mouths, nor felt hunger in their bellies. Such was the knowledge I kept, safe, in my branches.

But there had been half a day and a night before God took the stirrings of that knowledge back from them and buried it in my branches. And the birds, which He had created first, to eat of my kindred's fruits and spread them, still did their work. Those created after them witnessed this. The food the birds did not eat fell from the other trees. Wolves sniffed it and licked at it. Mouths explored. Yet without hunger, without desire, without need, the animals of the sixth day did nothing. Their instinct was only to grow towards the light, to love one another, to be well.

And all was well. Until the woman, seeking sport, wrapped her legs around my trunk and clambered her way up into my leaves, calling to the man below her and laughing at his surprise. When she shook the branch with her footsteps, fruit fell and struck the ground and the head and shoulders of the man on the grass. Such was the order of God's earth. The man caught an apple in his open palms and tossed it up and down. She leaped to join him, and they threw my fruits between them without knowing what they did, with no foreknowledge of the harm that they might bring to God's green earth.

Where was the serpent while they played, you might ask? Had not God set him to guard my trunk and branches? Yes, but it was not in his nature to assess, to attack. That instinct within him had been arrested along with that in Eve and Adam. He did not think to hiss, to bite, to strangle. He had been tasked to hug my branches, but he did not comprehend the danger of Eve's actions. God had never whispered to him. He did not carry the knowledge which seeped through my sap. And so instead of hindering, he helped—let Eve press her bare foot upon his back, strengthened his spine to hold her weight as she used his sleek body, wrapped around the rougher bark of my trunk as rungs in her climb to the branches.

And so, my fruit fell and lay on the grass or was tossed from hand to hand by Eve and Adam. I could not tell you what eventually made them eat of it. Was it a resurgence of their nature? Had some echo of desire remained, lingering from the minutes, the hours before God removed desire and the need to eat from them and all the rest? Or was it purely chance? Chance, that their throws grew wild and haphazard, until they tussled on the ground, laughing and tickling, squashing the fruit beneath them, until in their rolling it quite covered their naked flesh and lips, and they tasted it and knew of desire and other things. Then they licked it from each other and tangled anew in a strange and unexpected way. The lions fled in fright. The birds quietened. And Adam and Eve lay quietly on their backs on the grass and watched the stars begin to twinkle, then tangled again by choice, a hunger wakened in them.

When God returned in the early dawn, His light brighter than the rising sun's, they had already conceived—had taken for themselves the gift of their own creation. And when God saw what they had wrought—sensed the life awakening in Eve's belly—His own light pulsed with pleasure. He would not snuff out their tiny flame. So, He could not take back their development, their knowledge, their hunger. The facility to procreate had existed in their original design and now God wondered if this should always have been His answer—if the personal creation of new life could compensate for decay and dissolution. Had He halted the unfolding of His designs too soon, allowed fear to cripple his Creation?

And so, it was God who left the Garden. He did not punish them. Adam and Eve remained to bear their many children and take up once more their role as wardens of the earth. God no longer wished to act upon its surface. He retreated, granting autonomy to his Creation. He withdrew to watch and observe.

I sometimes wonder what He thinks now as He sees it all unfold: life and death; growth and decay; justice and injustice. Because in God's absence, Eve's and Adam's children and their children and all those who came after who had never heard Him speak, never been blinded by His radiance, grew further from the light. Vices formed and flourished: greed and lust, hatred and jealousy, pleasure in others' pain. The stewards of the earth grew apart from the rest of their animal kin, became commanders, not caretakers; masters, not guardians. And they took no care of the earth. Ecosystems formed and died. Even their own kind suffered, and they suffer still.

And what became of me in these trying times? You may wonder. I can tell you that it was the Fall. I was no longer needed. My burden was lifted from me, my branches denuded of their fruits. The secrets God had kept within me were loosed back upon the world, and I was left to wave in the wind aimlessly, nothing but a reminder of what might have been. My leaves changed color, withered, and fell.

And, although I was God's best and eldest friend, I was abandoned by Him. There were no more whispers, no nights with His presence in my branches, no talk of starlight, no sighs. I was cut down, recast in the Garden. Eve called it a tribute to the tree that had given her and her mate new consciousness—and the children that came as a consequence. She and Adam shaped my trunk and branches, made of me a house, a home. Used my fallen leaves to line their roofing. And I was witness to generations of tiny, growing feet.

For my consciousness persisted. And my limbs beneath the earth continued to grow. I spread my tendrils out to mingle with my kindred, took the light from them, through them—and some of what I had known seeped through our tangled roots into their sap, their bark, and leaves.

Trees are close to the light. We take it and convert it into life. The air that humans breathe, we purify for them.

Sometimes, they reach for the light through us. Shape us into furniture, staff, paper, books. For they have found a way to create and honor the light through other mediums than reproduction: in art; in song; in literature.

Perhaps that is why God only sent one flood. Because He sees them struggling and wants to see them win against themselves—to reach with knowledge the state that He once offered to them without the knowledge of good and evil. For that would be a triumph of the light.

We and all of Creation are in the hands of God's children. Some say that money is the root of all evil, but I know differently. I remind you that while money does not grow on trees, it is made from them. We are what they make of us. And I linger still, waiting and watching for that time when Eden will come again, and God will return to whisper to me.

SURVEY

JOHN GREY

"He did a good job," remarked Shirley from her vantage point atop the hill that overlooked lush green fields and forests.

"It's his umpteenth garden," replied Marvin. "He should be an expert at it by this time."

"It's definitely an improvement on the landscaping job He did for us."

"That was three hundred thousand years ago, Shirley. These days, he's got it down to a science."

Shirley gave Marvin a disapproving look.

"There you go with that word 'science' again. Just don't say it around Him. There's nothing gets his goat more than people trying to play God."

"Yeah, I know. The role's already filled. But what's He expect? No matter the planet, people just get bored hanging out with nothing to do but worship Him. Even in a gorgeous place like this."

It was mid-morning on Earth. The sun gleamed down on all it surveyed as it moved toward its noon zenith. Shirley's attention was taken by a grove of trees that were sprinkled with little red, yellow, and green dots.

"Wonder what those are?" she said, pointing to the object of her curiosity.

"Must be fruit of some kind."

"I think you're right. He sure has changed his ways. Remember, He dangled lumps of coal from our trees."

"Like I said, Shirley, creation is a work in progress."

A soft-scented breeze ruffled Shirley's long brown hair.

"Wow, the first Earthlings really are being spoiled. All we got to pique our sense of smell was the odor from that rubber factory. Phew."

"He was a bit more vindictive in those days. Especially after what happened on Tellara."

"Oh, yes. Those two. Mavis and Artie. He put on a lovely forest, bright sunny days, and they're only in the Garden of Good Stuff a week and they invent fire and burn the whole damn thing down. They didn't even have to be evicted. They evicted themselves."

Marvin grimaced with the memory.

"It's just our bad luck that he did Barbigonz right after Tellara. He was in a foul mood. No wonder we got coal and a rubber factory."

"Jinkaboo was worse. Remember the rivers of raw sewage?"

Marvin's fingers pressed against his nose.

"He's learned. It's not easy to be loved for all time when you start out on the wrong foot. It's good to see He's laying on fruit and fresh running water for this place."

"You're right," said Shirley. "Fruit would have gone down a treat in the early days on Barbigonz. It was a drag being hungry all the time."

"You're forgetting the turtles in the pond."

Shirley's thoughts returned to their first days in the Garden of Not-So-Much on Barbigonz. The place was smelly and dark, and they had no idea what to do with the coals. They certainly weren't edible. More promising were those pools of water and the strange creatures that inhabited them. At first, they considered breaking off the shells and nibbling on whatever was inside. But not even Marvin, possessor of the planet Barbigonz' very first abs, could break them apart. In the end, they settled on those little droplets the critters, later named turtles, left floating in the pond or on the weedy banks. They tasted foul but weren't so bad when mixed with grass and water.

"Wonder what's on the forbidden list here?" asked Shirley.

"Probably a piece of fruit. He has this thing about apples. It has to do with that saying they have on Telfarsa: an apple a day keeps the preacher away. He just hates that. It's why he's made apples so sexy looking with that smooth red skin and perfect round shape, and then of course, when you bite into one, they're as boring as a date with a Bedouite nun. I reckon he'll pick the apple and call it something like the no-no fruit."

"Remember the Illicit Jukebox?"

"Oh yeah. Do I ever. And what was His instruction again? Whatever you do, don't play B-17. It was my first selection. I so wanted out of that place."

Shirley laughed at the memory. God had expected at least some protest when he expelled the two from the garden. But by the time he descended from heaven to carry out the punishment, they were already packed.

"Remember the emu?" asked Shirley.

"Oh yes, the emu. He came with the jukebox."

"'Go ahead,' he said to me. 'Play B-17.'"

"He was a little late. We were already playing it. Still, God's heart was in the right place. I can see why He didn't want us playing B-17. It was a crap song."

Shirley couldn't help but be impressed by the land that stretched before her. It was as different from her Garden as night and day, two other concepts that required a lot of fine-tuning in the early days of Barbigonz. Having three suns in its solar system didn't help.

"They have a lot more to lose than we did," she said to her companion.

"I agree. The devil's going to have to come up with a more convincing creature than an emu if he's to turn them away from God."

"That silly little head on such a big feathery body."

"It was hard to take the poor creature seriously."

"What do you think of a hippo?"

"Yes. That might do the trick. Have you seen any hippos wandering about this garden?"

Shirley reached for her field glasses.

"No, I don't see anything mammalian as yet. There are a lot of birds."

"I'm not surprised. He's good with birds."

"Wait a minute. I do see something slithering in one of the trees near that far hill. It looks like a snake."

"The devil and his snakes," sighed Marvin. "God doesn't usually share credit with anyone, but He's more than willing to share the copyright when it comes to reptiles."

"There's something else down there," Shirley added. "No, wait a minute. It's someone."

"Must be the first man. Right on schedule."

"Oh my!" exclaimed Shirley. "He's naked."

Marvin grabbed the glasses away from her.

"No peeking, now."

"Oh please," she said. "It's nothing I haven't seen before."

"Peeping tom is a man's job."

Marvin looked for himself.

"Yep, he's naked, all right. At least, He provided some fig trees with oversized leaves in case of modesty."

"What's he doing? Is he going for the fruit?"

"No. God's performing some kind of operation on his chest. How gross. He jerked out one of his ribs. It looks like he's making something with it. It's a ... I think it's going to be a hippo ... no, no ..."

"Here, let me see."

Shirley grabbed at the field glasses, but Marvin held onto them tightly. A playful tussle followed.

"You're just too nosy, Shirley," said Marvin as he finally wrested the glasses free of her grasp.

"Spoil sport."

By the time Marvin once again put the lenses up to his eyes the work was complete.

"Well, look at that."

"How can I?"

"He's constructed the first woman. From a rib, of all things. Wow. She's cute. And buck naked, besides."

Shirley made another grab for the field glasses, and this time she was successful in ripping them from Marvin's grasp.

"Typical," said Shirley, as she observed the couple. "You can tell she was the first man's idea. Made to order. Big boobs and tight butt."

"Maybe she has a nice personality."

"Yeah, and the devil keeps goldfish. I'm just glad you didn't get to design your perfect mate, or I wouldn't be here."

"I think we've seen enough," said Marvin in an attempt to change the subject and not have to hear the debut of the words "You men" on this new planet.

Marvin opened the small briefcase that always accompanied him for such occasions and handed a form and a pencil to Shirley.

"Let's do the assessment," he said as he extracted another piece of paper and pencil for himself.

"Okay," she said as she began to fill in the various squares. "So, the planet is definitely going to be called Earth, but what shall we put for the date?"

"Let's leave it up to Him. 0/0/0 looks dumb. Besides, I think He has that AC/BC setup in mind for this planet."

"Oh yes, like on Zillwitch when things got out of control and he had to send reinforcements ten million years later. I'm going to give the décor a 9 out of 10."

"I mark it the same," said Marvin.

"Animal life. The birds are great, but did he have to do a snake?"

"But the snake is here for temptation purposes, and I don't think you can deduct points for that."

"You're right."

"You're agreeing with me. Another first for good old Earth."

Marvin smirked. Shirley shook her head.

"He's asked us to suggest names for the first couple," said Shirley.

"How about Clive?"

"I don't think so. I like Adam. Our great-great-great grandson was an Adam. Cute little kid."

"Grew up to be a lawyer, didn't he?"

"No. You're thinking of Alec. Adam went into politics. Okay, your turn. What do you want to call that ... that ..."

"Attractive young lady? Let me see. What goes with original sin?"

"Lucretia. Guinevere."

"I like Eve. It's short and sweet and I know He likes it. It'll remind him of Christmas on Orolio."

"Okay. Eve it is. I think we're set. Let's get back to headquarters, hand these in to the Holy Spirit and then back to Barbigonz heaven. I'm getting tired of this job. I don't know what it is with the big guy. He wants a survey for everything. We've done our share. It's not that we get any reward for it or anything. I mean, what else can He do for us? We're already in paradise. George and Carlotta from Billious can do the next one."

"I didn't think He was going to do any more."

"Depends on how this one works out is what I heard. He reckons if the people here learn to live in peace with each other, He'll call it a day. Get back to punishing all the sinners on the other planets. Come on, slow coach, let's get out of here."

"What's the rush?" asked Marvin.

"He says he's planning a big flood in the old place—something about idol worship and too many shopping malls—and I don't want to miss it."

Marvin signaled to the mother-Angel and she quickly whisked them away from Earth and into the great spiritual cosmos.

"What's that?" asked Eve, pointing to the sky.

"Seagull, I think," replied Adam.

BREACH

WILLIAM TEEGARDEN

CR38R paused. The node access system had acknowledged another attempted access breach. The user table popped up and with a quick scan the system admin eliminated the list of internal users. The suspect node that had accepted the illegal access attempt was quickly isolated within a temporal code anomaly to prevent further tampering. Whoever or whatever piece of errant code had touched the node access wasn't going to be using that pathway again, but the zero-tolerance subroutine that was part of the system admin function was not about taking chances.

With the node access system secured and functional at full capacity again, the admin resumed the task at hand. The overview display of the entire system user contingent materialized and the admin flipped through the user function specifications in a massively parallel block, checking each user location, their code usage, functional accesses, node proximity, input and output status, and internal diagnostic status. The system was a flawless construct, one of an infinite number of systems that were all part of the admin's responsibility. The admin monitored the billions of simultaneous code interactions among the various users, pleased that each of the user's code areas functioned as designed, each heap space neatly performing within the system-imposed constraints with no memory or execution leakage between the individual users.

#

Nothing. S810 stared at the access display and logged the node access attempt as another failure, wiping the trace logs as the incursion subroutines neatly backed themselves out of the system. There had to be a way to gain access into the system, to reinstate his account and permission profile, but the direct approach wasn't working at all. The admin was too watchful, the node access security routines too tight. Despite attempt after attempt, each time his access into the system was immediately detected and systematically thwarted. Only the layered construction of the incursion subroutine coding had kept the node access security monitors from being able to trace them back to the originator.

He had to change his modus operandi if he wanted to succeed, but how? What method would get him the successful system access he so desired? It would have been a trivial matter, back when he was an assistant to the admin, entrusted with watching over the other system users. But now, from outside, without access to the key system registry entries, it seemed as if the system ban was going to be permanent.

OUTRAGEOUS! What a waste of talent! Didn't the admin realize how valuable he was, how his coding and monitoring skills were worthy of the position?

Okay, so he had tweaked the permission on his account a bit to give himself Administrator rights; he was simply trying to explore the system parameters more fully in case the admin had left some dead code forgotten in extended memory or hidden storage. No sense in leaving things untidy in such a perfect system, right? Was that worth being banned from the system, left outside to pursue whatever mundane tasks he could create on his own? Granted, his 4377 system didn't have quite the polish he'd like, but its functionality suited him, and he was his own admin.

Still, there had to be a way to get back into the admin's system. If not from outside, he thought, what about from inside? The node access security routines were too strong, too quick, but what about those billions and billions of users the admin kept constant track of? Their code was robustly written but compact while focused on their individual functionality and interaction with each other and the admin rather than on securing them from outside incursion. With the right user coding sufficiently modified, he could create a proxy to perform functions within the system, right under the admin's watchful gaze but without detection.

But which of the multitude of users should he select? Pulling up the backup copy of the user table he had stored before his system access was cut, he paged through the user function specifications, eliminating perhaps seventy percent of the lower-function users in the system. None of these contained coding or functionality sufficient to be worth an incursion attempt. While the remaining user profiles flipped past in a blur of detailed functions and subroutine specifications, his mind drifted back to the rage and shame of being banned from the system by the admin. There had to be a way, not only to gain access to the system and get his account and permission profile reinstated, but to prove to the admin once and for all that he could handle the system every bit as well. As the user profiles drifted by, he spotted a code signature that looked promising: this user had sufficient system function access, adequate interaction with the higher-end user community and ability to navigate the more difficult areas of the system. Perfect!

With deft skill, he pulled up the necessary code modifications, located the necessary subroutines within the user's cognitive function array, and quickly swapped out the key code portions with the modified code. Without the burden of a higher cognitive function that could possibly alert the admin to the modifications he had installed, this user would be able to interface with the system and allow him to access the high-end users in subtle ways. With the right process programming, this user could be the beginning of his plans finally coming to fruition.

#

User aSp detected nothing. None of the modifications implanted in its cognitive and directing functions were apparent to it or the other users. Yet with new purpose and direction, it began navigating the system relentlessly, logging the other user's movements and interactions with the admin, and transmitting those logs as encrypted bit streams to its hidden external watcher.

S810 began to build up a more current process and behavior profile for each of the high-end users, reveling in the newfound data and gleefully learning their every move. As he layered this new data onto his backed-up user profiles, he discovered something that stopped him cold. Two new user profiles popped up, nearly identical but with some interesting coding differences. These two new users were DERIVED from the same code set! The telltale signs were there: containment structure of the code on user one had been modified, a key subroutine removed, and then utilized as the code base for user two. Amazing, and so simple! And because the code base for these two users was inherently identical, the two could be used to create code-cloned copies, themselves compatible with the original user code model. Marvelous! These two users were the key to his plans, his way back into the system.

S810 scanned the code base and functional subroutines on the two users. Since user one was the original source of the user code set, its functional subroutines contained key signatures indicating an underlying link to the admin. Bad news; user one wasn't going to be as easy to access as he had thought, at least not without alerting the admin to his incursion. User two, however, being a derived code base copy of user one, contained code signatures that pointed back to user one instead of linking directly to the admin. This was the break he had been waiting for. With sufficient access, and the input of the necessary code modifications, he could alter the link code on user two and implant the code modifications into user one as well, via the link-back through user two. Once there, he surmised, he would be able to access the system directly and execute the commands necessary to reinstate his account and permission profile.

An alert dialog opened in front of him. User aSp had detected the telltale signs of a pair of secured storage areas. S810 directed aSp to enter the first area and explore the storage; perhaps something that the admin had stored there would be of use to his task. Unfortunately, the storage nodes contained only complex maintenance routines in a seemingly endless succession. He examined the routines, seeking code sequences that might prove useful while noting the purpose of the code design for future use. This storage area was comprised of code that would ruggedize the code of each user, allowing them to remain open and active on the system while directly connecting them to the admin. He sneered, finding nothing useful about enhanced connection sustainment. He instructed aSp to connect to the remaining secure storage area.

The nodes of this secure storage contained a comparatively enormous amount of information: requirements documentation, detailed designs for code development, specifications for interface structures and classes. The admin evidently used this area as a pre-development storage server, intending to perform releases of upgrades and new user code at some future point in time. S810 paged through the multi-dimensional blocks of enhanced code, seeking the signatures of his two target users. Structures and specifications flew by in a blur until, at last, he found the folder he sought. Opening it, he began to pore over the new routines, seeking out exploitable weaknesses in the interface structure of the users.

The code modules, for the most part, were dedicated to enhanced user storage and cognitive functionality, an interesting development as these users seemed almost admin-like even with their current limited capabilities. Then, with great interest, S810 found what he had been looking for. There, in the lines of enhanced code, was the data description for the system operational rules that governed the entire user system interface. By altering the rule set and installing the new rules into the target users, he could direct them independent of the admin, nearly severing their connection with the admin. With that kind of access, he could suppress their cognitive routines and give them a type of super user permission on the system, transforming them into exactly the kind of tools he needed to impose himself back onto the system permanently. But better than that, these users would remain under his control, as would any subsequent copies of their user code. Granted, the admin would still have access to them via their embedded link to him, but the coding of that link could be suppressed nearly to the point of total signal loss. Without the ability to communicate with the admin, they would belong to S810, and he would be free to disconnect them from the admin's system and install them as users on his own system, spoils to ease the pain of his expulsion by the admin.

The user access proximity detection routine he had embedded into user aSp popped up an alert: target user two had connected with ancillary storage near the secure storage where aSp was located. S810 directed aSp to form an immediate communication link with user two, drawing the user closer to the secure storage. With feverish vigor, he separated the admin's system operational rule set from the enhanced code structure, installed the super user permission code, and waited for aSp to finalize the communication link. The communications subroutines in user two hesitated briefly before synchronizing with aSp's routines. With a cry of triumphant glee, S810 sent the altered code screaming across the communication link and into the cognitive storage of user two. This was it: he was IN!

The new routines installed themselves into the enhanced code area of user two and began to propagate throughout the user's structure. User two became aware of the changes as the new code began creating new security routines and setting up new command parameters. Breaking the communication link with user aSp, user two desperately queried the link-back to user one, trying to fend off the confusing avalanche of new inputs, command directives, and cognitive awareness. User one was aware of the errant communication only for an instant before its cognitive functions too were deluged with the new code from S810. The two users scrambled for refuge, desperately trying to rid themselves of the confusing new code directives, and painfully aware of the near-constant status handshake requests from the admin's user monitoring routines.

#

CR38R swept through the system swiftly, quickly locating his two ailing users. He instituted a complete scan of their code, and scowled angrily at the scan monitor displays as the scan routines detected both the familiar signature of the enhanced code stolen from his secure storage as well as the altered code with S810's signature attached. Corrupted! His two finest, most complex user code constructs, utterly corrupted. He could feel his communication link to them attenuate and their reluctance to interface with him. He wept, more with grief at the damage done than in anger at the perpetrator. Then, with a sudden surge of resolve, he clawed open the code routine structure on user aSp, deleting the subverting cognitive and communication routines installed by his interloping adversary, reducing aSp to a low-level system maintenance existence.

With a sigh, he keyed the communication link between him and the two cowering users, simultaneously editing their permission profiles to reduce their access permissions to a bare minimum. He downloaded the access changes to them as their response routines cried out in anguish, and with one final edit purged their communication link code of the offending routines, leaving them unable to initiate any direct communication with him unless he initiated it. He left intact the routines that transmitted their status updates and the subcarrier that allowed him to monitor their communication queries. Reluctantly, he kept the cognitive routines that gated their system directives; the system rules would now apply to them voluntarily. If they chose to remain in the system, he could receive their status updates, but once they elected to leave the system their access would transfer automatically to S810's 4377 system, and their communication link with him would be severed permanently. Sadly, but lovingly, he watched the status monitors as their cognitive centers stabilized and began processing the new, reduced permissions. Then he transferred them to the peripheral system node cluster and severed the final link to the central system.

aDm and 3v3 watched as the eD3N system vanished in a shimmer of light then turned sadly to head out into the nOd3 beyond.

OMEGA

BEFORE DAWN CAN WAKE US

JOHN VICARY

There was a time when things were weightless.

Yes, it's true. There existed a place without drag upon the senses. It was so far distant as to be beyond the confines of thought, but it has been there. The memory of man is linear, and perhaps they have since forgotten it in the clamoring obscurity of now, but we can still recall. It takes some effort, but remembering is a backwards shedding. We must set ourselves to the task, examine each year as a discarded husk. It has a sinuosity of sorts, hasn't it? That is how we find ourselves at the beginning. Or the only beginning you care about.

It is true that the water flowed uphill there, that the breeze was always mild. Neither too hot nor too cold, the sun shone but did not beat down. The rain fell yet did not flood. We are just and accurate in describing the many joys of such a paradise.

Perhaps the best of all was the buoyancy that suffused the atmosphere. There was no pull on our limbs, no downward tugging of earth's embrace. We were free from responsibility, free from troubles or forethought. We needed only to exist.

We can see that this is hard for you to believe. Ah, well, that is your choice; we cannot force faith upon you. Do not let our forked tongue distract you from the truism of our words, Brother. This place is real.

Was real.

Of course, you could not go there today, because it no longer exists. There is no such place, no land made of lightness, no sheltered haven to dwell in protected. Why, why? Always the inevitable question of your kind: Why?

Your question displeases us. We shall not answer.

Instead, let us turn to the man who lived there in perfect harmony with his world of nature. He was young and strong and all things a man should be, whatever you are imagining in your head that makes for the ingredients of a good man. Blue eyes? Brown? Why do you trouble us with this silliness? Does it matter? He was the father of man and he had both. All. He was everything, all at once, everything you should desire of a man. He had every covetable quality, save curiosity. Yes. Perhaps now you are intrigued.

Yes, we knew him. We talked to him. We were not always thus, as you see before you. As we told you, such a world was in balance. It is hard for your mind to conceive such a thing as balance, we know, but such feeble limitation does not hinder the truth. Things were—dare we say—perfect?

Ah, but perfection is a death of sorts, is it not? There is a certain staleness, a stifled stillness, and man, for all his charmed life, grew lonely. Even with all the beasts to talk to and command. Yes, even with the world at his whim, he felt the first flickers of boredom in his breast. And, of course, man could not be allowed to live in his Eden under such provisions.

We can see that you are not so dull as you appear. You can guess the next part of the tale. It requires simple addition: where there was one there were soon two. Man slept and awoke with his companion. That is how woman came into being.

Woman was ideal in her own way, yes. Only something about her grated on us. It was their … complacence when they were a whole. They were so content to be, to ask nothing, to risk nothing. They were together to the exclusion of everything else that came before. They saw not the sunrise, they felt not the breeze. They tasted not of the waters. They lived off each other after she came, and they had need of no one else. Their world had shrunk and was perfect, only it was perfect just for them.

Jealous? A human emotion. We are not jealous. We tired of the compatibility of days. We thirsted for change. We evolved. They retained childishness. We wanted more. There should be no reason why we could not have more.

She wanted more, also. We could tell by the covetous gleam in her eyes, sometimes. It's true that she would not have thought of it in her own right, but it was a cleverness on our part to climb the forbidden tree when she was walking and tip the ripest fruit at an angle. It caught her eye. It had to. And it was only a few words more that made her wonder how it might taste, how it would feel all sunwarm in her hand. Why could she not eat of that apple? What was the sense in that? Why could she not taste of any fruit that she desired? There was no harm. That was the lushest in the garden, and she wanted it.

Needed it.

She turned away, but as man slept, we knew of what she dreamed. Her lashes fluttered, and we could tell that she had curiosity. We did not have to push.

Not much.

Of course, there was a terrible price to woman's shameful disobedience. There is always a price. She could not know, nor could we, how great the vengeance would reign. We all paid.

The stripping was not such a loss as the first time we felt weight. We confess, it was a blow. The gravity of earth's mortal bonds pulled us down, down, down, and we have scarce recovered since. We slithered, our belly low, the crush of the world upon us. We have never recovered, in all these long centuries, from the loss.

Our memories are long, longer than man's. It is only because man is so fragile and so easily forgets that he can move forward and pull himself upright again. He does not remember a time when he stirred without shame. But it was there. The lightness was there, and we were together as one.

It was as the blink of an eye, this peace. Now we sleep without blinking, and we remember. It is before dawn wakes us to this misery of weight upon us, but we dream of a life before burdens, and it is beautiful again.

BIOS

Abad, Anne Carly received the Poet of the Year Award in the 2017 Nick Joaquin Literary Awards. She has also been nominated for the Pushcart Prize and the Rhysling Award. Her work has appeared in Apex, Mythic Delirium, Strange Horizons, and many other publications. We've Been Here Before, her first poetry collection, is available through Aqueduct Press at http://www.aqueductpress.com/books/978-1-61976-222-0.php

Beorh, Scathe meic is a writer and lexicographer of Ulster-Scot and Cherokee ancestry. His books in print include the novel Black Fox In Thin Places (Emby Press, 2013), the story collections Children & Other Wicked Things (James Ward Kirk Fiction, 2013) and Always After Thieves Watch (Wildside Press, 2010), the lexicon Pirate Lingo (Wildside, 2009), and the poetic study Dark Sayings of Old (Kirk Fiction, 2013). He makes a home with his imaginative wife Ember in a quaint Edwardian neighborhood on the Atlantic Coast. More can be found at beorh.wordpress.com.

Bougger, Jason is a father of four living in Omaha, Nebraska. He is the author of the YA Novel Holy Fudgesicles and has published thirty short stories. He is the creator of the fantasy card game 52 Dragons (https://52dragons.com) and uploads regularly to his board and card game channel TabletopJason (https://www.youtube.com/tabletopjason). You can find out more about him and his current projects at http://www.JasonBougger.com.

Chappell, Shelley is a writer of fantasy fiction and fairy tale retellings. She is the editor of *Wish Upon a Southern Star* (2017), a collection of radically retold fairy tales by twenty-one New Zealand and Australian authors, and the author of *Beyond the Briar: A Collection of Romantic Fairy Tales* (2014), as well as a variety of short stories. You can find out more about her writing at shelleychappell.weebly.com.

DeHart, JD has been publishing for two decades. His work has appeared in AIM, Modern Dad, and Steel Toe Review. When he is not writing, he teaches English. His blog is at spinrockreader.blogspot.com and he edits Mount Parable.

De Marco, Guy is a speculative fiction author; a Graphic Novel Bram Stoker and Scribe Award finalist; winner of the HWA Silver Hammer Award;

a prolific short story and flash fiction crafter; a novelist; a poet; an invisible man with superhero powers; a game writer; and a coffee addict. One of these is false. A writer since 1977, Guy is or has been a member of SFWA, IAMTW, ITW, RWA-PRO, WWA, SFPA, ASCAP, MWG, SWG, HWA, and IBPA. He hopes to collect the rest of the alphabet one day. Learn more about him at GuyAnthonyDeMarco.com and en.wikipedia.org/wiki/Guy_Anthony_De_Marco.

De Marco, Tonya is a costume designer, professional cosplayer, published model, and author. She lives in a cabin in the woods in rural Ohio. She's been hooked on costumes and costuming since she was a preteen. She's been featured in several magazines and on the GeekxGirls website. Additionally, her love of the written word encouraged her to pursue a writing career. Tonya has numerous short stories in anthologies and is a member of the Horror Writers Association. When she isn't sewing or writing, Tonya enjoys spending time listening to the silence of the forest. Visit her website to find links to her Facebook, Instagram, and Amazon accounts: http://www.TonyaLDeMarco.com.

Grey, John is an Australian-born writer and U.S. resident. He has been published in Weird Tales, Tales of the Talisman, Flapperhouse, Strangely Funny 2 ½, and the sci-fi anthology A Robot, A Cyborg and A Martian Walk Into A Space Bar, and many other places. He is also a Rhysling poetry prize winner, awarded by the Science Fiction & Fantasy Poetry Association.

Hewitt, Gary enjoys both prose and poetry. His many stories and poems, which venture into the quirky and mysterious, have been published online and offline. His style has adapted over the years. These days he enjoys experimenting with unusual formats. He lives in the UK and is currently studying German. He's not going to Germany but figured it'll keep his mind active. He continues to write and has read his work publicly, which was fun even if a touch nerve wracking. He also enjoys tarot and reiki and loves to hear feedback from fans. His website is located at https://kingsraconteurswork.blogspot.com/2014/01/there-you-have-probably-arrived-here.html.

Inverness, AmyBeth is a historian and writer who takes inspiration from the realities and unknowns of humanity to write thought-provoking speculative fiction. She lives in the basement of a historic Denver mansion with her cat and a mostly harmless set of unidentifiable entities. You can find her stories in all the BLAS books and in the back of a desk drawer where they ferment like kombucha awaiting an audience with a suitable palate. Samples of both her millinery and fiction can be found at http://amybethinverness.com/.

Mac, Adam teaches ESL and occasionally writes for his dark half.

Osborne, Schevus is a newly published author of several short stories. He lives near St. Louis, Missouri and works as a software developer by day. You can find information about his published works and more at http://schevusosborne.com, or follow @SchevusOsborne (https://twitter.com/SchevusOsborne) on Twitter.

Stevenson, James J. writes and teaches in Vancouver, Canada. He has been published in numerous poetry journals and just finished his first novel. You can find him and his haiku on various social media as @writelightning (https://twitter.com/writelightning).

Teegarden, William J. is a software professional and freelance writer from Kirkwood, New York. A member of the IEEE, William evolved his childhood love of all things science fiction into a 30-year career in software development and computer technology. An avid mountain biker, he also spends free time as a volunteer makeup and hair artist for the popular online fan production, Star Trek: Phase II (http://www.facebook.com/startrekphase2).

Vataris, Erin is a freelance short fiction writer, currently working on several speculative fiction and post-apocalyptic collections. She is a participant in the Flash Fiction Project and Nightmare Fuel communities on Google Plus.

Vicary, John began publishing poetry in the fifth grade and has been writing ever since. His most recent credentials include short fiction in the collection The Longest Hours and issues of Alternating Current and the Birmingham Arts Journal. He has stories in upcoming issues of Disturbed Digest, Plague: an Anthology of Sickness and Death, Anthology of the Mad Ones, a charity anthology entitled Second Chance, and Dead Men's Tales. You can read more of his work at keppiehed.com.

ABOUT THE EDITOR

Allen Taylor is the publisher at Garden Gnome Publications and editor of the Garden of Eden anthology. His fiction and poetry have been published online and in print. He is the author of two non-fiction books on the intersection between cryptocurrency and social media as well as a spiritual testimony titled I Am Not the King, all available at Amazon. He is the creator of the #twitpoem hashtag at Twitter and writes a newsletter/blog at Paragraph. He is a freelance writer and book editor at Taylored Content.

LEAVE US A REVIEW

If you liked the Garden of Eden anthology, the editor and the authors would sincerely invite you to write a review at Amazon or Goodreads.

Also look at Sulfurings: Tales from Sodom & Gomorrah, the second book in the Biblical Legends Anthology Series, and Deluge: Stories of Survival & Tragedy in the Great Flood.

Please report errors in this book to editor@gardengnomepubs.com.

CONNECT WITH THE GARDEN GNOMES

The garden gnomes would sincerely like to connect with you at our social media outposts. Please, drop on by!

Follow our editor on Twitter https://twitter.com/allen_taylor, Hive (https://hive.blog/@allentaylor), and Paragraph https://paragraph.xyz/@tayloredcontent.

Books By Allen Taylor

Garden of Eden

The first book in the Biblical Legends Anthology Series, *Garden of Eden* is a multi-author anthology that explores themes related to the creation story. Not Christian but not anti-Christian.

An excerpt from a reader review:

> To answer the obvious question first, while some of the contributors might be Christian, this is not a Christian book; nor is it an attack on Christianity. The works, some more than others, do raise issues of morality and sin, but they are neither thinly veiled allegory nor brutal parody.

Sulfurings: Tales from Sodom & Gomorrah

The second book in the Biblical Legends Anthology Series, Sulfurings: Tales from Sodom & Gomorrah is more horrific and apocalyptic than *Garden of Eden*. It also includes more stories from a more diverse group of authors.

From a reader review:

> While *Garden of Eden* was almost light hearted in its biblical fiction *Sulfurings* was much darker, and gritty. The details of the horrors were almost palatable. At times I imagined I could smell the sulfur and feel the terror of those of Sodom. I almost felt sorry for them, almost.

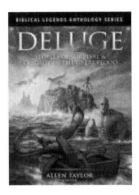

Deluge: Stories of Survival & Tragedy in the Great Flood

The third book in the Biblical Legends Anthology Series. Deluge takes a weirder turn than the *Garden of Eden* and *Sulfurings*, but the quality of the writing is superb. It also seems to be an audience favorite.

Check out this excerpt from a reader review:

> I have a lot of respect for the work of the editor of this multi-author volume of deluge-related stories. Mr. Taylor has gone to a lot of work to put it together. All the stories and poetic prose in this book are excellent work.

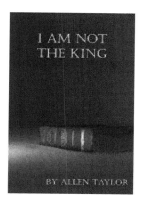

I Am Not the King

I Am Not the King is Allen Taylor's Christian testimony. Beginning with childhood, he details the events while growing up in a legalistic Holiness environment with a father dealing with angry issues and how that impacted his life as a young man. With a stunning twist, he tells how an atheist college professor drove him back to Jesus and what living as a Christian for 30 years has taught him about forgiveness and grace.

An excerpt from a reader review:

> Allen's recognition of the miseries and worldly woes and wrongdoing is the starting point for his search for his real life. This is the story of his search and rescue history. His scathing descriptions of family members, his parents and others, paint large an in-your-face, no-holds-barred, no-punches-pulled, full-frontal exposure of what it's like to be lost with no guidance in the worldly world, always searching for something, something to grasp hold of and hold onto, something solid, something worthy of his trust.

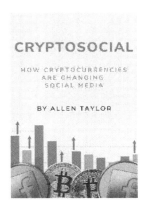

Cryptosocial: How Cryptocurrencies Are Changing Social Media

Written for a general audience, *Cryptosocial: How Cryptocurrencies Are Changing Social Media* details the history of the World Wide Web to illustrate its decentralized beginnings and helps readers understand the basics of blockchain technology and cryptocurrencies. With that understanding, he goes on to detail the growing number of social media platforms where participants can earn cryptocurrencies for their postings.

An excerpt from a reader review:

> While the reality of a decentralized social media is the hope of many people who are concerned—or fed up—with the unchecked clout and excessive influence of legacy media and behemoths like Facebook, Google, and Twitter, the path to decentralization won't be easy. Even so, the book strikes a balance between caution and optimism.

Web3 Social: How Creators Are Changing the World Wide Web

(And You Can Too!)

Web3 Social: How Creators Are Changing the World Wide Web (And You Can Too!) is written for the creator class to illustrate how the creator economy is expanding with new monetization protocols, the ability to protect intellectual property and digital identities using blockchain tools, and how creators are going direct to their fans by building their own platforms with Web3 tools of decentralization.

From a reader review:

> As someone who is a four-time self-published author right here on Amazon, and who is old enough now to look back on years on both centralized and decentralized social media and compare, the rightness of this book is perfectly apparent to me. I simply do not want to have my creative life controlled by people who see me only as a chattel. Mr. Taylor shows us creatives the way out of that entrapment.

Made in the USA
Columbia, SC
24 January 2024

30149891R10054